POR

THE MERMAID CHRONICLES

The Mermaid Chronicles

ROBERT HERNANDEZ

Sense of Wonder Press
JAMES A. ROCK & COMPANY, PUBLISHERS
ROCKVILLE • MARYLAND

The Mermaid Chronicles by Robert Hernandez

SENSE OF WONDER PRESS
is an imprint of JAMES A. ROCK & CO., PUBLISHERS

The Mermaid Chronicles copyright © 2007
by Robert Hernandez

Special contents of this edition copyright ©2007
by James A. Rock & Co., Publishers

Address comments and inquiries to:
SENSE OF WONDER PRESS
James A. Rock & Company, Publishers
9710 Traville Gateway Drive, #305
Rockville, MD 20850
E-mail:
jrock@rockpublishing.com   lrock@rockpublishing.com
Internet URL: www.rockpublishing.com

ISBN: 978-1-59663-546-3
1-59663-546-0

Library of Congress Control Number: 2007927816

Printed in the United States of America

First Edition: 2007

Dedicated

to my father

Roberto J. Hernandez

Acknowledgments

Regarding the Biology

I hashed out most of the biology for the mermaids through many conversations while attending the University of Miami. Four brilliant and particularly insightful humans whose brains I picked greedily stand out, and I would like to thank them for their guidance.

Dr. John DeLuca
Dr. Teresa Hernandez
Dr. Julian Lee
Dr. Rafael "Rafe" Ortiz

Regarding Grammar

My good friend, and extraordinary English teacher, Betsy Hutchinson scoured this story for grammatical inconsistencies. Given my shotgun approach to writing, her task was formidable. Her accomplishment is the stuff of legends.

Table of Contents

CHAPTER
1

A Month of Storms

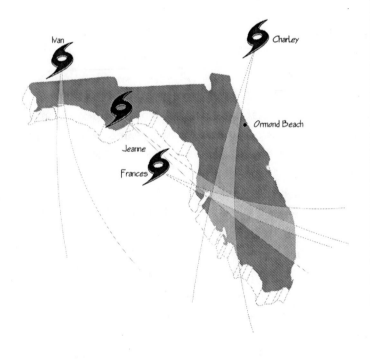

Storm Tracks through Florida, Summer 2004

Ormond Beach, Florida, August 2004

In what can only be described as a most peculiar month ... there was a storm. The storm wasn't the true beginning. In truth, it wasn't even part of the story at all. Had the storm not passed however, this story would not be known. So with a storm, it began.

A storm in Florida was not unusual. From monster hurricanes like this one was becoming, to the lightning-rich downpours accenting every summer afternoon, Florida has always had storms. Storms are the levy Floridians pay for living on a flat, beach-laden, fertile peninsula that never sees snow. The scientists who study weather use an alphabetical naming system to identify larger storms. Personalizing a swirling mass of water vapor with a human name seems silly, even to the scientists, but it helps with keeping track of them ...

They called it "Charley."

Charley was a big, raging, bloated leviathan that bullied its way along the Caribbean, beating up any helpless little islands unlucky enough to find themselves in its path—something quite difficult to avoid since the storm covered so much area and islands can't move.

Initially, Charley was quite far from Ormond Beach, Florida, the hub around which this story's events rotated. But that would soon change.

Wikipedia[1] describes Ormond Beach in the following manner.

Geography

Ormond Beach is located at 29°17'11" North, 81°4'30" West (29.286405, -81.074882).

According to the United States Census Bureau, the city
has a total area of 75.3 km² (29.1 mi²). 66.7 km²
(25.8 mi²) of it is land and 8.6 km² (3.3 mi²) of it is
water. The total area is 11.42% water.

The US Census of 2000 antiseptically portrayed Ormond's demographics in the usual myriad of sets and subsets. Wikipedia mentioned some of them. Specifically poignant to understanding
Ormond's heart was the following breakdown.

Demographics

... There are 36,301 people, 15,629 households, and
10,533 families residing in the city ...

... Of the 15,629 households, 23.5% have children under
the age of 18 living with them ...

... In the city the population is spread out with 19.2%
under the age of 18.

These statistics stated in numbers what the residents simply
knew—Ormond's a great place to raise a family.

Lacking a large employer, children were the city's principle industry. The focus of the entire community seemed to be on them.
Ormond Beach maintained a magnificent soccer and baseball complex, yet they sported no professional teams. The facilities were rec-
reational, predominately for the kids. PTA participation in the city's
schools was expansive and evangelical. The dozen or so parks dot-
ting the landscape were always packed and the public library sat on
one of the most lucrative chunks of real estate in town.[2]

Despite Charley's distance, the residents of the small coastal
community were nonetheless keenly aware of it. Thanks to the
marvels of technology and the high ratings disasters pulled—at any
time, on any date—they could turn their TVs to just about any

local channel and be greeted by a dour-faced weather forecaster's warning that, despite the great distance and all the other false alarms they had sounded over the years, THIS storm was different. THIS storm was serious. THIS storm would hit.

The forecasters, ecstatic with their instantaneous promotion from their trivial role as News Show Clowns,[3] basked in their camera time. Rather than their typical minor role on the summer local news—a two minute graphic-saturated narration of the incredibly obvious bordering on comic relief[4]—people actually tuned in to listen to THEM. With a sincerity characteristically attributed to religious figures, they insisted that disaster was imminent. Anyone near the coast (which in Florida meant *everyone*) was urged to immediately evacuate the state—but without panic and in an orderly fashion—using any of the two available roads.[5] And those handfuls who fell under the delusion that they were far enough inland to be safe were implored to fortify their homes for a siege. The forecasters, languishing in their temporary spotlight, reluctantly concluded their reports (and thus their air time) by staring hard into the camera so the viewer could sense the deep anguish in their souls. Then they'd qualify their apocalyptical predictions with a completely transparent whopper of a lie, "Well let's hope this one stays far away! Back to you Generic Anchor Man and Woman."

In the days that followed it became apparent that, unlike the many, many, MANY false prophecies of doom broadcast in previous seasons, this large swirling chunk of atmosphere with a goofy name did indeed bear them malice. Ormond residents took the news alert to heart and barricaded their homes with a forest of plywood. They cleared the canned food aisles, bought a lake of bottled water and a power plant's worth of batteries ... and they waited, monitoring the monster's approach on TV and the internet.

Gorging itself on the abundant power food for storms—warm tropic waters—Charley grew. With its expansion came power, so Charley grew strong. Tiny islands no longer posed a challenge. Even Cuba, the largest of the Caribbean land masses, succumbed to the storm's onslaught. On the island nation dictator's birthday, Charley made landfall, destroying many crops, pummeling the already hovelled city of Havana and ruining Fidel's party.

Pounding Cuba emboldened Charley, and it set out into the Gulf searching for a truly worthy opponent. Once back over water, Charley swelled to gargantuan size and strength. It teased several places for a bit, before eventually slamming into Southwest Florida with the finesse of a runaway freight train. Barely slowing after crushing Port Charlotte, it exploited the flat geography, careening deeply into the peninsula, hammering through Orlando, and popping out on the east coast just north of Ormond Beach. After running its destructive course, Charley lumbered off into the Atlantic waters that spawned it to wreak havoc on other coastal residents. Inhabitants of the "Lately, Not Very Much Sunshine" State emerged from their plywood bunkers to inspect the gifts this generous storm had left in its wake—rivers swelled to capacity and seeping over their banks, forests of felled trees, downed power lines, shredded billboards and millions of Floridians without the luxuries of electricity, cable, or telephone service.

And in Ormond Beach, there was one other gift. A gift whose impact would resonate throughout the entire world, long after the memory of the storm faded to the soft musings of grandparent stories. The Tomoka River, a gentle waterway, docilely meandering through the Ormond suburbia, grumbled restlessly. It had for decades been content to serve its function—transporting normal rain runoff from the region to the sea. But Charley had nearly instantaneously dropped a month's heavy precipitation into the system. What's more, civilization held a lower tolerance for standing waters than nature.

Storm drains sucked up rain with an efficiency nature could never hope to reproduce. Gutters led to drains which fed pipes which in hours funneled an entire storm's deposits into the river. Invigorated by the deluge, the Tomoka churned menacingly. Once, long ago, this river was not the sort where golfers chatted idly on its banks. Once, long ago, children would never have dared to navigate a flimsy, homemade raft in its waters. Once, long ago, it was a wild and dangerous river where no sane person would ever have built a house, let alone entire neighborhoods, so close to its shores.

Brimming with the runoff's massive infusion and goaded on by strong winds, the Tomoka River recaptured a bit of its early nastiness and pushed hard against the civilization that had tried to corral it. To the dismay of the river, the city pushed back harder. Ormond built its town quite well, leaving the waters no place to go but downstream. But there was so much of it now that the lazy river became, for a time, a roaring highway as the rising waters desperately sought a release to their overcrowding. Fast-moving foamy waves washed away the soft sandy banks, pulling in trees which suddenly found themselves with no soil to anchor them. Loose house parts, entire docks, and fencing fell into the river and they, too, were washed along. Boats left by owners who were certain they'd be "all right" joined them. An eclectic flotilla of natural and artificial debris made its way towards the Tomoka's mouth.

The waters slalomed through the city, maneuvering the handful of bridges spanning the banks; speed and sheer volume quickly resolving any bottlenecks created by the columns.

At Tomoka State Park, the river spilled into a basin. The basin, in turn, fed the much larger Halifax River, which was really the ocean seeping in behind the barrier islands where, on another storm landscaping job, the beaches were being ripped away. Here, in the broader and hence shallower channels of the basin, the inevitable occurred.

The cumbersome litter tangled. It started with one large tree on the park's shore losing its grip and falling over into the river. The tree jutted to within a few yards of a spoil island and jammed up a chunk of dock, which in turn trapped a few more trees, a capsized boat, some fence parts and anything else that came near it. The tree/dock/boat/fence contraption became a net, snaring smaller and smaller bits as the spaces between the parts clogged and choked with everything from twigs to slow fish. In a matter of minutes, the flow was stifled.

The Tomoka was dammed at this spot and quite unhappy about it. Building waters pressed hard to bring down the dam. Loud creaky snaps crackled in the air as the sloppy barrier bent, but would not buckle. The dam slid a ways but, for every bit of headway gained, a hundred litter chunks piled in to replace it, resulting only in tangling it even more.

Jams like these were common and temporary. The river always could and always did exploit other avenues. In tamer times, water would simply pool at the dam's edge, patiently waiting for the combination of erosion and weathering to clear up the inconvenient clots.

But at the moment, this was not a patient river.

The angry Tomoka, desperate to get past, violently ricocheted off of every facet of the clutter obstacles. Foamy water slabs leapt over in long crescents and jets shot through the mesh, blasting firehose style sprays of dirty water. Eddies gouged the bottom silt, digging a significant, but futile tunnel underneath ... and all the while still pushing.

Then the water found the spoil island's sandy shore. Unlike the dam, pushing here made headway. The bank, consisting of sludgy sand, rock and shell, provided little resistance. Water gushed into the island's "high ground"—which really wasn't. The already saturated soil dissolved under the invasion, obliterating the few scrawny pines and grasses that barely held on in calm times. The enormous deflected pressure easily carved a rut across what was—until this moment—a rather nice place for a picnic. Then the river met up with itself and continued its journey, albeit via a slightly different course. Waters behind the dam shriveled, absorbed by the thirsty, porous ground, leaving mucky soil that will someday be another nice place for a picnic.

So what was once a long, thin spoil island, was now a short, thin spoil island with a rather messy jetty nearby.

Rivers often change course so, like the storm, this also was not very unusual. In fact, centuries before, this particular piece of land had undergone an inverse metamorphosis—all the land between the shore and the island had been dry. The river submerged it.

The inhabitants who once dwelled on the newly-exposed land had long ago abandoned their homes, taking great care to hide that they were there at all. They were thorough, but their technology was primitive and their vision limited, so they concentrated their concealment to the superficial, relying on the Tomoka to blanket the rest. Deeply buried under what was once the center of their village, they left something behind. Nearly half a millennium ago, an angry bitter debate on whether to take it with them was fought on this soil. The Council House rattled with the argument for an entire night. The verdict was an assortment of hurt feelings and a decision that the Secret belonged not with them, but on this land. They masked the site, bid their farewells and left the Secret hidden under many feet of sand, confident that it would be safely concealed for eternity.

Nature however has a way of making a mockery of what humans consider eternal. Shortly after they left, the waters of the Tomoka shifted. Perhaps it was a storm, or the intrusion of a particularly high tide, or another jam. Perhaps it was something unnatural. The diversion's cause was irrelevant. That it *occurred* was undeniable because where once there had been the sandy banks, only dark water remained.

The river instantly set out to uncover the Secret. Grain by grain, over the years, the gentle but persistent Tomoka current flicked away the piles of sand. Mineral-laden water, pushed downward by the weight of the river above it, seeped through the earth to the Secret, replacing the soft, brittle molecules that comprised it, with the dense hard stuff of statues. When finally the sands were cleared away, the Secret was transformed to an impermeable thing that could easily resist the chipping of a mild current. It rested on the bottom, a cryptic memorial of something cherished by a people who had long since disappeared.

The river's revelation was its own. Submerged as it was, only the Tomoka and its underwater denizens knew of the monument.

Then—as was stated earlier—there was a storm.

With the waters taking an alternate route, the Secret was laid bare under the hot muggy summer sun ... exposed in plain sight ... and begging to be discovered.

For only when it was found, could this story commence.

Unfortunately, the chaos this storm inflicted meant that the Secret had to wait. Ormond, like most of Florida, was a mess. A battalion of power company cherry pickers descended into town to restore civilization. Cranes and dump trucks crisscrossed neighborhoods collecting stacked litter piles. And the residents, wielding brooms and chainsaws, tidied their communities. In a short time, employees returned to work, restocked stores opened, schools restarted, and life was nearly back to a level of normalcy ...

Then there was another storm.

This one they named "Frances." It came from the East, crawled ever so slowly through the state, crossing Charley's earlier path and forming an "X." Frances was weaker than Charley, but infinitely more annoying because it was slow ... EXCRUTIATINGLY slow! At one point it even *stopped* for a spell. And while Frances strolled casually across Florida, it rained ... and rained ... and rained. Floridians hunkered down in their once-again powerless homes, darkened even further by the plywood décor, and waited for the annoying storm to go away.

Outside, the Secret was further exposed, scoured clean of its dirt and grime by Frances' persistent rainfall. It laid there, a beacon of revelation. But again, it was to wait, because there was more clean-up to do. Ormond residents swept the new batch of shingles and leaves off their sidewalks, as the now familiar cherry pickers made their rounds. They followed the news cautiously as a third storm teased for days before veering off to decimate the Florida Panhandle.

Ormond breathed a sigh of relief along with a prayer for their northern neighbors and returned to their brooms and rakes. Finally, after two weeks, Ormond was back to speed ... again—power restored, folks at work, plywood stored, and schools open. The sun even came out a few days, long enough to evaporate some small puddles and to bleach the Secret a shade or two whiter.

Then, ridiculous as it sounds ... there was another storm.

Hurricane Jeanne was a surprise even to the forecasters. It had turned away from Florida and was trudging harmlessly to its death in the cold Northern waters when, like a cat that suddenly realized it just had to be in another room, Jeanne pulled a 180-degree loop in the middle of the Atlantic and headed due west.

Storm-fatigued Floridians prepared yet again. In one of the few cases where procrastination paid off, some folks had been so busy with other work that they hadn't taken their plywood down. They were in essence PRE-prepared. Regardless, Ormond residents, along with the rest of Florida, completed their all too familiar drill, and they hunkered down to endure yet another onslaught. The storm came,[6] drenched, battered, and left, following Frances' route across Florida. Mercifully, Jeanne was a speedster. It cruised through the state quickly. Other than stealing several million tons of beach, it left Ormond cluttered, but relatively unscathed.

Another round of rakes, chainsaws and cherry pickers later, and the distinct possibility of a hurricane-free weekend actually seemed possible.

After a month of storms, the first sunny Saturday was met with a ravenous flair. The weather had cooled just a bit. It was still hot enough to melt Northerners but, other than Canadians, and surfers in wetsuits, there weren't many folks in the water. Besides, everyone had enjoyed plenty of water lately. It was the sun they hadn't seen. Ormond beaches were crammed with sunbathers, volleyball games, soccer, football, and people just checking out the newly formed cliffs carved from what used to be gentle dunes. What they did was irrelevant. It was being outside basking that mattered.

The parks were slower to accommodate visitors. They had more trees down, but they too welcomed the claustrophobic families trying to get some sun.

Tomoka State Park in particular had some trouble. The densely packed trees had formed a tremendous snarl over the three-storm barrage and the swollen river had shifted some waterways. But, in the spirit of providing their facilities to the town, they opened their gates. The museum, the marina, and the restaurant were still closed, so there wasn't much to offer, but the river was good for fishing, and the bank slope was gentle enough to launch a canoe.

People would come ...

People would wander ...

And the Secret waited...

It would be found.

CHAPTER
2

Mister Gomez

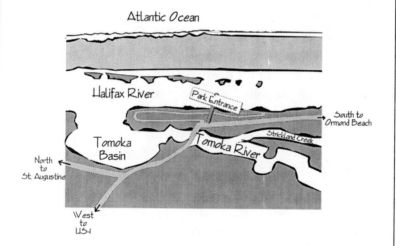

Tomoka State Park, Ormond Beach, Florida

Manuel Gomez enjoyed fishing as much as his wife enjoyed church—and for pretty much the same reasons. Fishing was a spiritual experience. Most of his fondest memories involved fishing. Whether it was standing with a tiny donut reel between his father and his uncle at the crooked pier; his rare, but exhilarating boat trips on the Atlantic; the day he was old enough to abandon the donut reel and hold an actual rod himself; repeating these experiences with his now grown and married children, or any of a thousand little moments of happiness; it didn't matter. They were all good.

Fishing on Sunday morning and going to Chili's Neighborhood Bar and Grille with Elena—his wife of forty-eight years—on Wednesday nights were the highlights of his week. Manuel was a custodian at David Hinson Middle School. He was seventy-two but, since he looked younger than he was, and birth certificates did not exist in the small coastal Mexican town where he was born, immigration had shaved off twelve years of his life when he obtained his green card upon entering the United States in 1970. He would therefore not be eligible for full social security benefits until his seventy-seventh birthday.

This bureaucratic glitch was common knowledge and irked Manuel's coworkers to no end. They continually urged him to file all sorts of appeals to correct the record. Some activist teachers had even introduced him to an attorney willing to take the case *pro bono*.[1] The slender, quiet custodian with a pencil thin mustache and slick black hair that refused to go grey, always listened, always thanked them, but never followed through.

In truth, he didn't want to retire. Manuel enjoyed the work. The kids, many from affluent professional homes, were a bit pampered, but they were polite mostly. A few of the teachers lingered in their classrooms and chatted with him as he swept and emptied trashcans. To break the monotony, Manuel carried a small tool belt and performed light maintenance in the rooms he was assigned. This endeared him to no end amongst the teachers. Touched by the spontaneous, unsolicited assistance, Manuel's rounds were sprinkled with little gifts—cookies, cake, donuts, sodas, gift certificates to Chili's, notes of gratitude, and even cash. Teachers came to rely on him as a shortcut to solving problems the cumbersome physical plant of public schools would never get to. He regularly entered rooms to find pleas for help written in perfect penmanship on the chalkboard:

"Manuel, the fourth desk on row one is a death trap."

"Mr. Gomez, could you check the storeroom light? It's flickering."

"AAAH! Manuel, the sinks grumble every time we turn the water on."

"Manuel please … That confounded third window blows open every time the wind picks up!"

Manuel would fix what he could and relay the few outside his expertise to his supervisor. His job provided good health care for him and his wife. It paid the bills and still left enough for Wednesday's dinner and some very good fishing gear. Any doubt he harbored about his circumstances was disintegrated during the confinement of these recent hurricanes. After just two days he had run out of things to fix and was driving his wife insane. She nearly shoved him out the door when the school finally called the custodians in to clear the campus after each storm.

Today's fishing trip was the first since August. Manuel had chosen Tomoka State Park as his destination because he had heard it fared poorly in the storms and wanted to see for himself. He got a clue on how poorly as he drove up Old Dixie Highway to the entrance. After passing the neat grid of Ormond neighborhoods, the modest two-lane road which connected Daytona Beach to St. Augustine for over 400 years, darkened considerably. The dense tree canopy announced that Manuel had crossed the park perimeter more effectively than the most elaborate of signs ever could. Cleanly-cut stumps and visible sky splotches were everywhere, evidence of both the storms' toll, and the efficiency of the clean up crews. The park gate was open, but there was no one at the little booth to collect the admission fee. Manuel slipped the three dollars under the door and drove on.

Navigating through a slalom of forest litter the rangers had bundled together to await the rubbish trucks, he eventually parked at the marina, took his gear out and headed along the Tomoka River shore in search of a good casting spot that had some shade. The hiking was difficult. Felled trees jutted into the water, creating a steeplechase course he was forced to traverse with a rod and tackle box. Something seemed wrong about the river too.

He had not been inside the park for a while, preferring to save the admission fee and fish on the bridge just outside the entrance. So he wasn't certain, but the flow of water seemed light, especially after all the storms. Manuel vaguely remembered that he had fished along this area before, but because of the altered geography, he was uncertain. In any case, fishing here would be impossible now. At its deepest point. the bottom couldn't have been more than a few inches. And noting that skinny barrier island just north of the bridge, about a hundred feet from the shore; he could walk to it now. That wasn't possible before. He was pondering whether it was his memory or the river that was off when, after scaling a particularly large horizontal pine, he found his answer.

The river had been turned. Not far, but enough so the waters that fed the span between the shore and the island were drying up. An immense and disorganized dam, assembled by either insane beavers or a hurricane, had choked off flow. The waters had turned and carved an escape through the island itself.

Now Manuel saw that there were two islands where, very recently, there had been one.

"*No, todavia es una isla*"[2] he corrected himself. If he could walk to the second island, then it really wasn't an island anymore. With that observation, Manuel found his fishing spot. He checked his rubber boots, tucking in the pant leg bits that had escaped during the hike, and squinting, stepped into the sun, onto what used to be a river.

He began his walk to what used to be an island. The span was slick and cobbled. Rocks of sizes varying from gravel to boulders glistened with moisture. Some, where algae still clung, were treacherously slick. Strewn throughout were pockets of standing water that on inspection were over a foot deep. Aware that a twisted ankle would ruin his trip and force him to be home for an extended period with nothing to do, he proceeded with extreme caution. The going was slow but he was in no hurry and the novelty of walking on a riverbed distracted him.

Manuel noted that the rocks bore the pebbled shape indicative of moving currents. He was surprised to find so little silt, but reasoned it must have been washed away in one of the storms. Remembering it was Frances that brought down the most rain, he guessed the dam must have occurred in the first storm. He noted from the bald pebble tops that much of the algae were dying and reasoned that this had more to do with the salinity than anything else. This portion of the Tomoka was brackish. Algae accustomed to the saltiness probably suffered with the fresh water rainfall.

"*Que cosa mas interesante. La agua dulce esterilizo las piedras,*"[3] he mused.

Wondering what other interesting bits the dried riverbed would reveal, he examined the area. About two-thirds of the way to his fishing spot, standing out against the brown pebble background, Manuel spotted a larger white object. About the size of a football, too spherical to be a rock, the mysterious object was curious enough to justify a diversion of about a hundred feet. As the distance decreased, Manuel saw that there were other smaller, but similarly colored objects extending from one side. Three steps later, he finally pulled the visual clues together.

He'd found a skeleton and, judging by what was now categorized as the skull, a pretty big one too. A deer or wild boar perhaps, or maybe even a large raccoon or a family dog. What had the hurricanes killed? The orientation of the figure was such that he did not discover the amazing answer until he was nearly upon it. When he did, a dramatic shift in the egotistical perception humans had of their role in the molding of this planet occurred.

At this moment, finally, the Secret which had for so long been kept tightly hidden by the river, was revealed. For the first time in over five hundred years, the eyes of a Land Tribesman fell upon a Child of the Sea.

But Manuel did not know this. He thought he had discovered the skeleton of a rather tall, dead person.

Adrenaline-stoked panic ran for a bit through his veins before reason brought his pulse down. His initial conclusion was that he had found a hurricane victim. He tried, but failed to recall reading about an Ormond resident missing from the storms. There were no unaccounted people as far as he could recollect. Besides, the bones were clean and bleached. Both processes took a lot of time and the hurricanes had been so recent. This could not possibly be a hurricane victim.

Manuel's brow furrowed with worry as the next explanation came to mind. He had lived through his share of crime, and this unmistakably dead body resonated with malice. Many explanations—mostly recaps of crime dramas he had watched on TV—went through his mind, setting off yet another panic attack. Manuel, now overcome with a desire to make sense of his find, ignored the warnings of those very shows against tampering with the crime scene and … he tampered with the crime scene.

Using a towel from his tackle box, and a nearby pocket of relatively clean water, he cleared the remaining sand off the bones to see what it was he had truly discovered. He had no idea what he was searching for … a bullet? A large knife jutting from the ribs?

As he cleaned, it became more and more apparent that this was an old death. The bones were very hard. They were obviously fossilized and almost half of them still embedded in rock. He quickly readjusted his thinking from detective to archeologist. Who could this mysterious dead person be? An early settler drowned and submerged until now? A fisherman perhaps? A runaway slave? Maybe a soldier deserting the civil war … He wished he had a more thorough understanding of Florida's history. But like most of the state's sixteen million residents, he knew about Ponce De Leon, the Cuban Missile Crisis, the 2000 election and not much else.[4]

His preoccupation with cleaning and daydreaming kept Manuel's mind distracted until the skeleton was as exposed as he could get it. Therefore, rather than trickling suspicions, the full impact of what he had unearthed hit him undiluted.

"Dios mio, no puede ser!"[5]

He had to be mistaken. It was a play of light, or some trick the river pulled in the arrangement of bones. What he saw simply could not be. Manuel was a practical man, and could not accept that he was looking at something truly impossible. Not convinced at what was obviously glaring at him, Manuel stepped back, walking around the skeleton so he could view it from a different perspective.

It didn't help.

That he had unearthed a grave was undisputed. From the skull down to the ribcage, the skeleton was undeniably human, lying with arms folded in a manner familiar to anyone who had attended a funeral or seen vampire movies. Below the pelvis, rather where the pelvis *should have been,* a secret—THE Secret—hidden from the people of the land, finally connected. Manuel had never attended high school, but he cleaned the science classrooms and he did have cable. He had therefore not only seen skeletons on the Discovery Channel, but he was loosely aware of the names and function of each bone.

This was not a "normal" skeleton.

There was no pelvis or, if there was, it was a mere shard of what it was supposed to be. He guessed that what was left of it must be that fat lowest vertebrae on the spine. There was a hint of some type of hip crest, but the shape was extremely miniaturized and compacted. A sole femur, a bit smaller than Manuel thought it should be, jutted from two sockets on that pelvis/vertebrae thing. A barely perceptible groove running its length hinted that there might have once been two distinct bones here but, as it was, they fused into one shaft immediately upon exiting the socket. Only one lower leg bone—the big one he thought was called "tibia"[6]—was visible although the other—the "fibia"[7]—could have been embedded underneath, inside the rock.

This bone, too, seemed smaller. And there was a third, long bone between them. It was stunted, less than half the length of the tibia, and shaped funny, as if it were made from material that wasn't originally long. The three bone distances combined end to end, forming what appeared to his eyes to be a disproportionately long lower body.

"*Pero, con que puedo comparer?*"[8] Manuel exclaimed, bewildered.

The single heel was comprised of many little bones, and was very thick and compacted into a knobby ball. The "feet" were grotesquely flattened and spread fanlike. Each toe, the pinky in particular, was incredibly long. Manuel was unsure why a skeleton would have only one leg, yet two feet until the pieces casually reworked themselves.

It was not two feet at all ... it was *one* tail.

He knew this shape. He knew its name. He had seen cartoons, movies, and had even driven with his children to the famous Weeki Wachi Springs[9] tourist spot to see women in costumes designed to look like this put on slow moving underwater ballets. Breathless, barely above a whisper, he branded the skeleton, uttering what it undeniably was aloud, speaking the impossible ...

"*Sirena!*"[10]

Now the discovery was complete. A Secret *uttered* was a Secret *revealed*.

Manuel sat on his tackle box and, for a very long time, contemplated what to do next. Ignoring the find and continuing with the day's fishing was out of the question. For a while, he played with the notion to reinter the body. This was, before all things, a grave and he had been indoctrinated long ago to leave all dead things alone.

There was also the matter of desecration. Those who deposited this body held sufficient regard for her (him … it?) to undertake the ritualistic placement. He had also been taught to treat cemeteries as hallowed. He'd feel terrible if it were desecrated.

But the discovery of a mermaid, even dead and fossilized, trumped his trepidations. Of course he could be grossly mistaken about the bones. There might be a perfectly good, but non-fantastical explanation for the deformities, but he doubted it.

"*Que devo de hacer contigo sirenita?*"[11] he asked the bones, his hand lightly, almost protectively rubbing the dense ball of the skeleton's tail as he spoke.

Manuel finally accepted that someone needed to be told of this find, and determined that his best course was to report it to the rangers. They seemed like a good bunch whenever he ran into them. Silently hoping his impression was accurate and that they would treat the grave with the appropriate reverence, AND the knowledge that there was nothing he could do about it if he were wrong, Manuel relaxed somewhat. This discovery was not a burden he had sought nor, having attained it, did he enjoy bearing it. It had ruined his fishing time and if the rangers disappointed him, this could possibly weigh his conscience down in the coming weeks. He was eager to be done with it and go home.

"*Bueno, por lo menos, me has dado un cuento interesante para Elena esta noche.*"[12] he told the bones, patting the tail affectionately.

He rose to depart but hesitated. There was something elsee his conscience was nagging him to do. From his shirt pocket, Manuel removed the one item he always carried close to his heart—his mother's rosary. Other than his clothes and an extra pair of shoes, it was the only thing he'd brought from Mexico. So, donning the sign of the cross, he prayed a rosary for the soul of the deceased, tracking the prayers with the well-worn beads. A volley of "Hail Marys" later, Manuel reholstered his precious rosary.

Aware, now, that there was little chance this skeleton was Catholic, he stood over the bones for a bit, thinking of a brief eulogy. All he could come up with was;

"*Ojala vivistes bien sirenita.*"[13]

He marked the site by digging out a hole with his knife and planting his rod with the towel attached like a flag.

He never got around to fishing that day, but he most assuredly had quite a story to tell his wife when he arrived home late.

CHAPTER
3

Ranger Jane

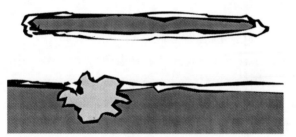

Before the Storms:: One Long Island

After the Storms:: One Short Island and one Jetty

Manuel wandered through the park slightly disoriented and a tad uneasy. There was nobody in sight. Other than his car, the parking lot was empty. The buildings around the marina were locked. Ordinarily the solitude would have been welcomed by a fisherman, but with the weight of his discovery pressing on him, he anxiously sought another human's presence to lighten or, hopefully, remove the load.

He did not recall seeing anyone along the road as he drove in, so he followed it deeper by foot. Slipping over and around the horizontal trees strewn across the asphalt, he walked on until he detected the duel sounds of muffled profanities and grunting coming from a spot in the forest. He finally found a ranger.

"*Bien fuerte.*"[1] Manuel noted. She was a strong girl.

"Ranger Jane" Peterson was dragging a tree branch that must have weighed over one hundred pounds with her thickly gloved hands. Manuel's initial reaction was one of concern over the red-haired woman's horrible sunburn, but he relaxed (only a little) when he realized the redness was from exertion, not the sun. She was in her early forties from his estimate, quite fit, the short-sleeves, grey Florida Ranger shirt and long green pants highlighting her very well-toned physique — a testimonial to the heartiness of a ranger's lifestyle. Her long, red hair was pulled back into a sloppy, wet ponytail which was probably quite taut when she began her labors earlier, but was now twisted to one side and barely hanging on. Bands of straggling hairs had escaped their scrunchy confinement and were now mortared with sweat on her fair, lightly-freckled cheek, partially obscuring a pair of piercing jade eyes. Her work boots were so heavily caked in mud and leaves that Manuel could not distinguish where the boot ended and the pant leg began. He waited for her to deposit her load next to the twenty or so similarly-shaped branches — once part of a rather large live oak — and for her skin to return to its fair-freckled hue before approaching.

Jane was the head ranger and the only employee on duty that day. For most of the week, the park had been teeming with workers, both ranger and civilian who, bleeding and sweating took on the Herculean task of clearing the grounds so they'd be accessible to patrons. They had toiled without complaint under muggy hot weather and through countless rain showers. The results of their labor, while incomplete, were quite remarkable. It was still battered, without many of the amenities and pockmarked with mountains of forest litter, but Tomoka State Park *was* open today.

After working for thirteen days in a row, she had given the staff a respite for the weekend to attend to their personal affairs. Jane volunteered to run the park alone. She chose to do so out of gratitude for their efforts, but she had her own selfish reasons as well. This weekend was one of the very rare times that her ex-husband actually showed an interest in their daughter.

Saundra McFarlane, a fifteen-year-old, straight "A," Spruce Creek High School sophomore, who had lettered in just about every women's sport at the school, was in Tallahassee for a Florida State Seminoles' home game. She and her father went every year and hung out at the campus where Jane and her ex had met and fallen in love.

They always had a reasonably good time together, then he'd be too busy to see Saundra again until around Christmas. Saundra shared more than her mother's athletic interests and complexion; Jane knew her daughter's soul because she was a miniature version of herself. Saundra was aware that their weekend together was a hollow gesture and that her father only did it to show off his intelligent, attractive daughter to his fraternity buddies. But she was, despite her appearance, still a child and a child needed her dad. If she couldn't get the complete package, she'd make do with what she had.

Jane didn't know whether she disliked her ex more for taking Saundra this weekend or his more predictable neglect of her the rest of the time.

So Jane dove into the park clean-up in order to expunge the worry over her daughter's feelings from thoughts. She'd been clearing brush all morning, and welcomed the interruption by the excited old man. She listened patiently and followed Manuel to the find, never suspecting that there was any *true* reason for his excitement. Her working guess was that a decomposed dolphin and a vivid imagination had come together with the morning sunlight to create an illusion she would patiently dispel.

The old man made light conversation and Jane contributed the occasional "uh-huh" in response but, essentially, Manuel was talking to himself because Jane was, for all practical purposes, in Doak Campbell Stadium[2]. When Manuel suddenly stopped and pointed down, her attention returned to the moment. She found herself standing over... it.

Jane visually examined the skull and scanned downward. Her eyes locked on the tail and would not blink. Quietly gaping at the find, allowing her mind to digest what it was seeing, she realized that one thing was certain — this was NOT an illusion.

She owed the old man an apology.

Without taking her eyes off the skeleton, Jane backed away towards the shore.

"Mr. Gomez, I'll be right back. Can you stay here please?" she called as she began to speed away. Manuel indicated that he could, but he was talking to a red ponytail. Jane was gone.

She raced to her office, ransacked the closet and her desk, threw the armfuls of materials into the bed of her truck and left a quarter inch of rubber on the parking lot as she peeled out. Jane sped to the park entrance with an urgency often seen on video games but never experienced by her old Ford, dodging the litter piles and checking for cars in the handful of parking lots along the way. Good fortune was with her. It was quite early on a church day and the park's status wasn't common knowledge. Manuel had been the only patron. She screeched to the gates, slammed them shut, closing the park again. It bothered her to do this after the sweat her staff had poured into getting the facility useable, but circumstances were such that she needed to control the environment ... to protect the find. People were simply too unpredictable.

Looking up and down Old Dixie Highway was slightly reassuring. It was completely empty of cars. Only an "Indian Run" of bicyclists in their bright, colorful "Please don't run me over" garments was visible heading north towards her. Bicyclists hardly ever entered the park. They flashed by in droves, running a 22-mile circuit nicknamed "The Loop" that would take them through both banks of the Halifax river, crossing at High Bridge (which really wasn't very), and the Granada Bridge (which was).

On the other hand, some cyclists were under the impression that ambiguous signs like "Park Closed" and "Keep Out" applied only to those nasty, internal-combustion transported folks, not wholesome, healthy, spandexed athletes like themselves. Jane needed to discourage such intrusions today, so she took some poster board and tape from the truck and, with a permanent marker, scrawled:

... Because of massive sewage backup

She affixed this directly beneath the permanent *Park Closed* sign.

She stepped aside and waved politely as she waited for them to pass. The fifteen or so men on this ride went through identical facial shifts—smiles to flirt with Jane, concentration to read the poster, fear upon realizing what it meant, then eyes front followed by a rapid increase in velocity. They darted past her and were soon no more than colorful distant dots.

There was no one else around. Jane got back in her truck and returned to the discovery. Grabbing the digital camera she'd tossed in the back, she walked past Manuel to again inspect the skeleton. The camera was expensive and relatively new, a donation from a resident who launched his boat at the marina. At Jane's prompting, its two-inch view screen crackled to life. She zoomed the viewer on the tail, but did not take the picture. Instead, through the restricted perspective of the tiny TV set, she slowly panned the image.

Her mind was in tumult. She was fighting the dueling presences of the unquestionable observation her *eyes* made and the outright impossibility her *mind* knew. It appeared that she was better able to meld them if they were ingested in small, rectangular morsels.

Yet unconsciously, she kept whispering. "No way … no way…"

Resting on a pine trunk, Manuel followed Jane's movements. Rather, he watched her changing expressions since, other than the slightest tilt of the camera, she was frozen in position. Her face was contorted with a wild mixture of emotions, oscillating from confusion to shock, to embarrassment, to frustration, and eventually settling on … what? Serenity? Peace? Awe? A confusing expression set in at the end which Manuel could not place, yet he was certain of its presence.

He was feeling it, too.

Perhaps it was a revelation? A hidden spark in their minds had been ignited. In an age where technological marvels are the norm; where people carry cell phones as powerful as Star Trek communicators; where every letter of the human genetic code has been mapped; where the very edge of the cosmos is photographed and the pictures made available online for school children to access … pure, unqualified wonder was a vanishing emotion. The magical was expected and delivered daily. This evening the skeleton before them changed all that because, apparently, once, long ago, on the Earth, on this very spot … there were mermaids.

Unusual for the times and fortuitous for humanity, neither Manuel nor Jane were interested in the glory and financial gain that amazing discoveries promise. These temptations never even crossed their thoughts. They burned with a much more powerful energy, one that is rarely mentioned, but has fueled all breakthroughs since fire—*curiosity* for answers. Jane finally snapped out of her stupor and took charge of the scene. She was the head ranger after all.

With Manuel's assistance, they sealed off the area using orange construction mesh. After some photographs to record the site,[3] they draped a blue tarp over the skeleton, weighing it down with stones so it would not fly off and then retired to the ranger station. Jane produced two Coca Colas from the refrigerator and they sat ... and sat ... and sat.

Neither knew what to do next.

They agreed someone had to come in to study the *find*, but could think of no one to call. They did have a very good notion of who NOT to call. Alerting the television stations and the local paper would undoubtedly result in the grave's desecration. Either the press would do it in an effort to get a good picture or it would be trampled by droves of curiosity seekers. They also ruled out calling the police. If anyone had committed a crime on the owner of these bones, they were no better off by now anyway. The police would undoubtedly contact the press. Calling the National Park Service, the Smithsonian, local governments, even the FBI were also ruled out. Activating such a large entity could be incredibly embarrassing should they be mistaken in their conclusions.

"It is a scientist who needs to come here. A scientist can examine *la sirena*[4] and tell us if we are being foolish," Manuel finally suggested.

Jane agreed.

Using the single computer connected to the internet as a reference, they each took a phone and called the biology departments of the state's major universities. Sifting through the notoriously sluggish campus bureaucracies on a Sunday was even more frustrating since they agreed that openly explaining their predicament would be futile. Jane tried once anyway;

"Hi, um ... We found a mermaid skeleton, and—"

CLICK!

"Hello?"

Asking less direct questions, they managed to acquire the name of someone potentially quite useful. At the University of Miami, a paleobiologist—Bernard Sherban—appeared an ideal match for this puzzle. Versatile, talented, and very prolific (if the abundance of Google™ hits was any indication) Dr. Sherban had run some rather eclectic studies. While quite varied, his interests tended to focus in precisely what they sought—archeological physiology. As they read the synopsis of his other work involving both human and animal remains, Manuel and Jane got a sense that he was more like a detective than a scientist.

The UM website listed him as an active teacher, having just returned from his most recent work in Mexico. Dr. Sherban had analyzed the jumble of toad skeletons found around the altars in various Mayan Temples to determine if the owners were related to the modern species that secreted a hallucinogen[5] on their backs. There was a hypothesis, working through expert circles, that the fall of the Mayan Empire was caused by poor decisions made by addicted toad-licking high priests.[6]

More importantly, Dr. Bernard Sherban was within driving distance.

When they called, the science sleuth was not in his office, but the good professor had left his cell number on his answering machine for those students with urgent questions who were unable to wait for his scheduled hours. Jane held a college degree and had some graduate credits. She confessed to taking school (work, sports, life, etc.) a bit too seriously, but she could not imagine any academic question so urgent as to require such an immediate reply. They exploited the number's availability anyway, leaving a message.

One by one, the inquiry lines dried up. Jane kept track of those with promise on a legal pad. There weren't that many.

The ranger station's windows were still boarded up, so they were surprised, upon exiting, to see the day was winding down. Jane invited Manuel to go to dinner and discuss the find further. Manuel declined. He had spent the entire day here, much longer than his usual fishing hours. His wife would be worried. He asked that, if it wouldn't be too much trouble, he'd like to call the park next week to learn if she found any more information. Jane said it would be no trouble at all. She walked him to his car and, thanking him profusely for what he discovered, bid him farewell.

Jane returned to the office, grabbed her bag and keys, and was nearly out the door when the phone rang. She hesitated before taking the call. This had been a mind-boggling day and she did not have much energy left to handle a new crisis. She longed for a hot shower and a quiet night watching DVDs on her sofa waiting for Saundra to get home. She would exploit that down time to figure out what to do next. The discovery would distract her from worrying about her daughter. Lightning had incinerated the park's answering machine, so the phone just rang on and on. She hoped as she hesitated that the caller would tire and just hang up...

But the ringing continued, and Jane was compulsive.

"Tomoka State Park Ranger Station, May I help you?" she rattled off.

A deep melodic voice introduced itself as Bernie Sherban. He had checked his messages, and would be happy to assist. Coincidentally, he had just left Orlando and was on Interstate 4 headed for the Florida Turnpike and his trek back to Miami. Since he was not much more than an hour away, she took a chance and invited him to dinner and to check out the find. To her excited delight, Dr. Sherban accepted. They agreed to meet just south of Ormond in Daytona Beach at a local favorite, a riverside restaurant with good, inexpensive food and live music called "The Wreck."

Jane gave him the simple directions.[7] She described herself as "the only woman in the restaurant with a ranger uniform on" and they hung up.

If she was saturated before then this new development put her in overload. She had just asked a total stranger out on a date ... Well not a *date* date ... more like a meeting. With a pretty handsome guy if the internet picture was accurate ... at a romantic restaurant ... overlooking the water... around sunset.

Thankfully, there were no other rangers on duty to give her a hard time. She was constantly rebuffing their social offers, preferring a quiet night with Saundra to a drink with colleagues after work. Her lame excuses, had created a little resentment and her somewhat deserved reputation as a loner. Ever the naturalists, the rangers had concluded Jane was indeed a social butterfly, but one currently trapped in the pupae[8] stage. She wondered what her staff would think of this "cocoon" now that she was off to a "meeting" with a man she only had spoken to for thirty seconds.

"Can this day get any weirder?" she mused shutting down the office.

Jane liked The Wreck so, after the mandatory guilt pangs on how quickly she had made "her move" on the professor ran their course, she drove over to wait for him. The hostess seated her at an ideal table—right by the water, but far enough from the band for normal-voiced conversations. She ordered a beer and watched the boats skim over the Halifax River with the cover band's acceptable version of "Hotel California" playing in the background.

An argument about what Sherban would be like tossed and turned in her head;

"He's going to be a hippie,"

"No he's not, I saw his picture? He's kind of cute."

"Hippies can be cute."

"He'll be a nerd. I won't know a third of the words he'll use."

"But still, that picture ... he'll be a cute nerd."

"A cute, hippie nerd, who'll know I'm an idiot for thinking this ordinary skeleton is a mythical creature! What in the world am I doing?!"

The schizophrenic internal banter continued as she picked at her appetizer. Unaccustomed to the driving habits of Miami residents; Jane was astonished that Dr. Sherban arrived before she finished her beer.

His appearance fulfilled every "hippie" expectation—tan, bearded, thick, long, graying hair pulled into a loose ponytail and he wore scruffy jeans and sandals. His voice was deep, but not unusually so. The words he spoke were complex, melodic, and intricate, His "nerd" component was there as well.

And Jane could not deny he was quite handsome.

"Hi, I'm Bernie Sherban. You must be Ranger Peterson?" He shook Jane's hand. It was nearly as calloused as hers.

"Yes, hi, it's um ... Jane. Please take a seat," came her awkward reply.

They ate dinner, enjoyed an above average sunset on the river, and talked about what Manuel had discovered. But they also talked about what Miami was like, and Ormond, and research, and rangering, and Saundra, and why Sherban thought he'd never have children and why that was not necessarily a bad thing. They discussed movies and beach erosion, tourism and the Everglades; Led Zepplin and The White Stripes. It was a nice … time.[9]

In future interviews, reporters would question how trivial it seemed to complete their meal so casually with this spectacular discovery waiting. Their reply would forever be that the Secret had been buried quite a long time. In the great scheme of things, a few hours would not matter. And, they were hungry. Besides, who's to judge that a discovery is more imperative than a well-made meal and stimulating conversation?

After dinner (which Jane insisted on paying[10]) they drove to the park.

At the site, Dr. Sherban stood idly while Jane retrieved some work lamps from the office. She had forgotten to bring the camera, but she described what Manuel had found, and what they thought it was. Sherban was sure the two were mistaken. Certainly he would find bones, but upon a quick visual analysis he would gently correct the outlandish conclusion this layman and woman had made.

They had unearthed a twisted dolphin skeleton or perhaps a part of a manatee or whale, or maybe it was human, but with another animal's bones mingled. He agreed to help them because he rather enjoyed the idea of community involvement with the university. Surrounded by colleagues immersed in their research and students obsessed with their GPA, he found it quaint that an eclectic pair like these two in a tiny state park near a town he had never heard of shared the passion for knowledge which had started him on this career.

Jane lit the lamps, pulled back the tarp, and stepped back. Dr. Sherban glanced at where the beams were focusing and, with gaping jaw, he too became a believer.

Dr. Bernard Sherban stared at the skeleton for a very long time. Somewhere in the back of his mind he was aware that Jane was

smiling triumphantly—basking in the satisfaction that she was jus-
tified in thinking this discovery was important. He knew he should
address her, but that would have to wait.

Cautiously, as if he feared the bones would scamper off if he
approached too quickly, Dr. Sherban reached over to inspect the
tail. Marveling at the elegance of adaptation and the simplicity of
nature, he noted that the feet had been converted to tail flukes in
much the same manner that bats evolved wings. One toe—the
pinky—acted as the principle support arch and the others reinforced
the middle. The heels were much thicker than a tail center should
be. Was this a weapon? Did this creature—probably a *merman* rather
than *maid,* judging by the broadness of the shoulders —use his tail
as a bludgeon?

The leg bones—recast as a tail—were gnarled with deep indentations—tuberocities—where attached muscles yanked at bone. He
must have pumped his flukes up and down like all the other sea
mammals and exerted a tremendous thrust as he flexed. He noted
that the patella was elongated and sandwiched between the femur
and tibia. And, rather than its traditional role as a hinge, it had
been converted to another long bone for the tail.

Questions came in waves, too fast for him to consider for more
than an instance.

How evolved was this creature?

Was this the end state for the tail or would there be further
refinements? Would the merman have fins on its back?

How did he breathe? Was he actually able to pull oxygen from
the water, or did he still breathe air?

Thoughts, questions, hypothesis after hypothesis swirled dizzy-
ingly through his head. He was rapt with the connotations and had
to be snapped back to the present by Jane. Dr. Sherban vigorously
thanked her for calling him. He assured her that this indeed appeared to be what they believed it was and, after answering all the
questions she cared to ask, requested that she remain for a moment
while he made some telephone calls. Jane checked her watch and
reluctantly agreed.

Sherban, utilizing his cell phone, interrupted the biology department chair's date, who in turn interrupted the university president's fundraising dinner, who then interrupted an influential university supporter's fourth attempt at obtaining the phone number of a cheerleader half his age, who then interrupted the governor's quiet evening watching football, who didn't mind one bit that the university wanted to take some fossil samples from Tomoka State Park to their labs as long as they were returned eventually.

Sherban made a few more calls. He asked Jane for a good hotel recommendation. She paused, and without making eye contact, she nearly whispered, "If you don't mind the mess of two busy ladies, we have a spare room. You are welcome to stay with us."

An uncomfortable silence followed. Bernie was taken aback. This was certainly not Miami. He found Jane's invitation irresistible, especially since the blush on her cheeks nearly matched her hair. Bernie had been in work mode from the moment he got the call from Jane and only now, when she reddened, did he make any distinction regarding the consequences of her gender.

He initially wanted to decline, merely from his sense of propriety. But he reconsidered. Had this head ranger been a man, he wouldn't have hesitated to take advantage of the opportunity to work so closely with someone holding detailed knowledge of the site. Additionally, if this find panned out to be what he suspected, the accolades for the discovering party would be phenomenal. By turning down the offer, he would create a complicating barrier between the rangers and the university that need not exist. Worse still, he would in a way, be practicing a passive form of gender discrimination. And that would be seriously unfair.

Besides, Jane was quite interesting. He had enjoyed the dinner immensely and looked forward to returning the treat. Despite the mud-caked ranger garb and the tasseled hair, (or perhaps because of them)he had not missed observing how attractive she was. She had most graciously invited him, a virtual stranger, into her home. He would very much enjoy working with this person.

Yes, he would most gratefully accept her hospitality. To do otherwise was… rude.

Agreeing that it was best to leave Bernie's vehicle at the park, they transferred his bags to her truck and she drove them home. Saundra and her father were waiting at the door. They had only been there for a few minutes but the Seminoles had lost, and he was in a bad mood. Quick, brief, uncomfortable introductions were made. Disapproving looks exchanged, and Jane's ex-husband left in an even worse mood.

Inside, Jane pulled out the digital camera and, with Bernie Sherban narrating at her side, she introduced Saundra to the merman. Saundra was tired. The ride back had been long and silent, but she was quickly energized when she truly grasped the fantastic images. Unlike the adults, she completely bypassed the denial phase and accepted absolutely the merman's existence. Her reaction was the perfect blend of maturity and excitement. Bernie marveled at the insightful questions she asked. Many of them he was mulling himself. He was also quite amazed at the similarities between mother and daughter.

Physically, Saundra was a younger, petite, "perfect reproduction" of Jane. Hair, complexion, eye color, even the freckle pattern matched. But, it went much deeper. They had the same inflections of their voice. They both exuded the same steadfast optimism, and energy. Their mannerisms were identical. At times, they even nodded their heads in synch. They had both welcomed him unquestioningly. Ever the biologist, Bernie needed to categorize and evaluate this unique relationship. His bachelor knowledge base again failed him and his pop psychology repertoire was nil, so he settled for what was familiar to him. Jane had mentioned during dinner that she and her ex broke up when Saundra had been five. They'd been on their own since then. Saundra was therefore a sampling of the results Jane produced after an intense decade of work.

Not bad.

After the slide show, Jane grabbed some bed sheets and went off to prepare the guest room. Bernie opened his duffel bag and pulled back. Even Saundra, who was across the room, smelled it. If there was a clean garment in there somewhere, the fermented sweat permeating in the incubated environment had stunk it up several hours ago. Quickly zipping the bag, and a bit embarrassed that, had this been his *own* home, he would not have been bothered by the odor, he asked Saundra to show him the laundry room. Saundra took him and stood by, nodding in disapproval, as he bypassed the sorting process and dumped his entire bag, whites, colors, and even the canvas duffel bag itself into the washer. Bernie added detergent, and switched the machine on.

When the muffled sound of pouring water indicated he had been successful, Bernie turned his attention to Saundra. She had been waiting for him to have a free moment.

"What happens next?" Saundra asked.

"The rinse cycle." Bernie replied smiling. Saundra returned the smile

"And in the morning, with your clean professor outfit ready to go, what happens?" she repeated not skipping a beat.

"I think I mustered everyone even remotely involved with the biology department. They're gathering the necessary equipment to secure and analyze the site. They should be driving up right about now. We're going to extract the merman and he'll be transported to the university, hopefully by tomorrow. I can do a lot more in my lab than at the park."

"Can I tell my friends that Mom discovered a merman?"

"I'm afraid not. Sorry. I'm pretty sure this is legit, but as a scientist. I don't have the luxury of going with my feelings. If word gets out before the validity of the find is confirmed, we're going to have a mess. Saundra, I don't know if you're aware how special your Mom and Mr. Gomez are. They did a tremendously noble thing contacting me. So many folks are out there looking for their fifteen minutes of fame, or a quick buck. Kind of a miracle really that neither she nor Mr. Gomez tried cashing in."

Saundra checked Bernie's face for any trace of mockery. She found none. He was genuinely impressed with her mom.

"So you're impressed because they did the right thing?" she asked.

"Yeah, I guess I am. Sounds sad when you put it that way, though." He started to leave, but added, for emphasis. "Look, you really can't tell anyone. Not yet. Not until we triple- and quadruple-check every possible angle to make *sure* this is real. Otherwise, it'll deteriorate into another Bigfoot or Elvis sighting. Both the university and your Mom will look stupid for taking this seriously. Then there'll be a media circus as well."

"Don't worry Dr. Sherban. I understand." she reassured him and bounded off to settle herself in.

"Neat kid." Bernie thought. Considering her tightness with Jane and that she'd been out all weekend, he expected her to be... what? Imposed? Cranky? Sarcastic? He realized he was woefully uninformed regarding teen behavior and really didn't know what he expected her to be like. But it was certainly not this intelligent cheerful person. It made him feel bad, insisting she keep this find to herself until the proper moment, but she had taken it well enough. Bernie made a mental note to make sure he included Saundra when the find was made public and that subject closed.

The rinse cycle kicked in and he took notes on his ever-present legal pad while waiting for the washer to finish. When the tub finally came to a stop, he dumped his entire "machine washable," "wrinkle free" wardrobe into the dryer and went to bed.

In the morning, a team of Dr. Sherban's bleary-eyed graduate assistants, along with an archeologist colleague, and several campus vehicles including an RV weighed down with all sorts of exotic equipment borrowed and/or stolen from a dozen other departments, arrived on the scene. Bernie and Jane were waiting for them with coffee and bagels. In four hours, a high resolution 3D Ground Penetrating Radar[11] scan revealed that there were no other hidden artifacts.

In that same interval, a second crew, running an electromagnetic survey,[12] found an unusually high concentration of iron oxide, but not much else.

Assured that the scene was clear, they enveloped the exposed bones in a protective plaster casing and brought out the explosives. Three carefully-placed charges later, a very special block of rock wiggled free of its ancient resting site and, with a jeweler's precision, was lifted onto a truck bed sporting a computer-controlled hydraulic suspension. Before sunset, the precious cargo was headed south on I-95.

Bernie remained long enough to introduce Jane to his team. Coordinating with her, they were going to run a gamut of tests around the remainder of the park and partly into the river, on the off-chance that there was something else. It would take about two weeks. His people were very competent, as was Jane. Bernie didn't need to be there and the greatest puzzle of his professional life was headed to his lab. Jane noticed he was looking at his watch way too often and offered to walk him to his truck. Bernie agreed so loudly, the grad students misinterpreted it to mean he was eager to be alone with Jane.

Or maybe they didn't miss it after all.

They covered the distance between the site and the parking lot on foot without a word exchanged. Bernie pitched his clean duffel bag into the passenger seat, again thanked Jane profusely, and started the engine to go when, without knowing exactly why, he suddenly stopped.

"Listen," he told her, stepping out of the truck, "I'm going to be saturated with this for a little while. I'm guessing you are too, for a few weeks anyway. But once things calm down, I'd like to return your hospitality. Would you and Saundra be interested in coming down to Miami? I can show you around. You can stay in MY guest room, and I can buy *you* dinner. Interested?"

Jane didn't answer out loud at first. Her mind screamed "YES!!!" but even these amazing events were not enough to wear away years of stifled spontaneity. The best she could do was to say, "I'll talk it over with Saundra. Call me when you're free, and we'll see."

Bernie liked that response. They shook hands and he drove off. They were both smiling like school kids.

Jane returned to the grad students and, after assigning them a small conference room in the back of the museum as a base of operations, they mapped out their search strategy.

After school, Saundra made a rare park appearance to see what was happening. She seemed disappointed that she had missed Bernie, but perked up when Jane told her of the invitation. She stayed long enough for Jane to introduce her to Bernie's team and then bolted to soccer practice. That night, over spaghetti, they discussed the find, Bernie, and Miami.

Dr. Bernie Sherban beat the merman to his lab. He spent the lead time preparing a room for the block and by Tuesday morning, he was working to free the bones.

***

In the weeks that followed, an army of lawyers armed with the deep university pockets, closed out the loose ends. Manuel signed an agreement with the university which awarded him hefty "finder's fee" compensation in exchange for his silence. He kept his custodial job but now, in addition to the Wednesday's dinner at Chili's, he also went to Applebee's on Tuesdays. And when he fished, it was on his john boat with its 5hp electric motor.

Jane was also compensated and within a month actually went on an "official" date with Bernie. She and Saundra began making frequent weekend trips to see Bernie in Miami. Occasionally, Saundra's schedule didn't permit her to join them, so she'd spend the night at her friend's and Jane went "unchaperoned."

Despite the first-hand knowledge that her Mom was staying in Bernie's guest house *alone*, Saundra teased her incessantly about "how the neighbors were starting to talk." Jane blushed, as usual, but enjoyed the razzing. It meant that Saundra liked Bernie almost as much as she did.

Tomoka State Park, through the work of the governor who took the word of several well-connected supporters, was awarded a reconstruction grant to speed up the recovery and to build a monument and information center. The latter was to be unveiled when the promised return of the remains occurred. In exchange for the financial and political capitol investment, the University of Miami gained initial rights to the discovery of the millennia.

And the world went about its business waiting to be changed.

CHAPTER
4

Dr. Sherban

Bernie Sherban's lab was located in, by his own admission, quite possibly the ugliest set of buildings in the country. They most certainly held that unquestionable title on the University of Miami campus. And that was the way he liked it. Nestled within a grove of banyan trees, the white, wooden bungalow-style series of shacks, a leftover from the very early university days, smacked in stark contrast to the sleek, manicured, concrete leviathan that was the Science Building. There had been, and still is, a subtle, but steady move by campus administrators to rid themselves of these eyesores, but Bernie wouldn't have any of that.

Like Arthur Dent lying in the mud, preventing the bulldozers from leveling his house,[1] Dr. Sherban was the lone obstacle to the campus landscape cleansing of all things not comprised of imposing concrete and glass. Had he kept any of them, Bernie could have papered the peeling walls with memos "inviting" him to select an office within the four-story, windowless structure designed by either an Iron Curtain architect or someone quite sympathetic to that style. Bernie's stubbornness, supported by his reputation, successfully deflected the multiple forced migration attempts.

He *liked* the bungalows. The banyans and porches provided a cool, outdoor workspace. They were out of the way, so he wasn't perpetually distracted by colleagues or administrative interruptions. And they were so shoddy that he and his staff could do literally anything to them without filling out a requisition. Over his tenure, walls had gone down to get stuff in and out. Scaffolding, shelves, pipes, electrical, even entire buildings were rearranged to accommodate the tools of the latest project. Bernie's favorite "adjustment" was when, over a weekend, he and his staff spliced three bungalows together, creating a long assembly line.

At the moment, however, only one project was underway.

Stretched out in an anatomical position[2] on a cadaver table stolen from the medical school was the extracted skeleton of the merman. A surgical lamp, the single light in the room, hung sloppily over the bones. An array of computers with SETI[3] screen savers lined a wall. A large, burgeoning bulletin board took up most of another. Strewn between the ubiquitous Far Side cartoons, highlighted with Post-It notes, were the clues to this latest mystery. Bernie worked best when he could see everything and this bulletin board strategy had proven, over the years, to be the most effective technique.

Sipping his third shot of Cuban coffee, Bernie paced. Occasionally, he'd pull a document off the wall for a closer look or he'd run to a computer, wiggle the mouse to clear the SETI screen and on the file he wanted ...

But mostly he paced.

It had been six months since Jane originally called him. He and his staff had learned so much.

Carbon isotope testing had dated the bones at around 500 years old.

Dental analysis had determined he was in his late twenties or early thirties.

X-rays had revealed a broken arm and a fractured skull. The skull injury appeared to be a fatal blow.

Reconstruction techniques had assembled a face that was most definitively Native American.

He was big. Six feet one or two if he stood on his tail.

He was strong and left handed.[4]

Bernie was working on the 500-year-old murder of a big, pretty active, left-handed Native American merman. That answered a myriad of questions but, like all science, it opened up a whole new set.

So Bernie paced.

His frustration was palpable. His usually relaxed demeanor had ebbed over the months and was now vanishing altogether, replaced with a quiet, polite intensity. His crew of graduate assistants no longer clowned around with him. He wasn't a jerk about it. He simply wouldn't return the banter they lobbed his way. Even Jane had threatened she'd stop coming down if he didn't lighten up. He just wasn't good company.

The only person who seemed oblivious to his mood change was, of all people, Saundra. The daughter of his ... what? Girlfriend? Ladyfriend? Woman he was seeing? Saundra seemed completely unfazed, blasting past his aloofness as if it were merely a poor choice of wardrobe.

With that, Bernie finally found the first of only two distinctions between mother and daughter. The other was their sleep cycles. Unlike Jane, whose ranger lifestyle had her snoring by ten, Saundra—like Bernie—was a night owl. Bernie exploited the quiet late hours, catching up on work he didn't do because he was enjoying the company of the two Ormond ladies. Saundra, took the quiet time to dive into her monstrously large textbooks and crank out her homework assignments.

During breaks, with Jane asleep on the sofa, they raided Bernie's freezer and enjoyed great conversations over Publix Butter Pecan Ice Cream on the kitchen counter.

As a result, Saundra was the only one who knew precisely why he was such cranky company—mainly because she was the only one to whom he had confided his problem. He had told her last night. He didn't mean to. She had simply caught him off guard and he just blurted.

After five minutes of silence at the counter she simply asked, "What's been up your behind lately? You used to be really cool. I mean, you're *still* cool, but you used to be really REALLY cool. Are you turning into one of those intense postal worker guys?"

"The kind the neighbors tell reporters, 'He was a quiet man?'" he asked, smiling.

"Yeah, one of those."

Bernie assured her he wasn't and that the vast majority of postal employees—his mailman in particular—were soft-spoken and quite even-tempered. "What's more ..." he continued, about to begin a distracting conversation thread on stereotyping-by-profession, when Saundra saw right through that ploy and would have none of it.

"If you're not going "postal," or "ballistic," or "nutso" or whatever the term for paleobiologists who *lose it* is... What *has* been up your behind then?"

Bernie was quite cleverly boxed in. So he simply told her. The slowness of the science didn't bother him. Neither did the appearance of more questions. That was the nature of his work. Bernie's frustration was that the data and the logical lines of research were pulling him further and further away from the one question he wanted most to know. From what he had managed to uncover, the merman was quite healthy. The teeth and bones were well-formed, micro-scans of the tissue had revealed no signs of disuse or malnutrition. Until the mysterious head trauma resulted in his sudden demise, Bernie imagined the merman was swimming quite successfully, a perfect adaptation of the human physique to an aquatic environment. And therein laid his problem. Perfection didn't just burst into existence. It took many many generations to hone.

Where were the others?

He had named the merman after a sea-dwelling comic book character he read a lot as a kid—"Namor the Submariner."

Where were Namor's parents? Where were his grandparents? And *their* grandparents? He was old enough to be a father. Did Namor leave a widow and children? Where were they? Where was Namor's village? Did he even have a village?

Given the magnificence of the discovery, Bernie knew it was sour to complain that more evidence didn't exist, but he couldn't help it. He craved to pursue the notion of Namor's species, but without another source to corroborate, he was forced to treat him as an anomaly. He was unable to even make a strong guess what body of water Namor lived in.

Namor was found buried, respectfully, on land. Native Americans must have done it. Given Namor's eccentric appearance, they may have considered him a water spirit or a god; or maybe they themselves killed him, thinking Namor was an omen of evil, and moved the remains far from their lands as a precaution. They might have transported his body for hundreds of miles.

Bernie had reached a dead end. Sifting the scientific data banks for other clues and the queries he pursued through historical records had all ended in unreliable myths and fables.

Bernie was therefore confined to the analysis of a single organism. A case study—albeit a magnificently *interesting* case study—that never addressed the true repercussions.

"Doesn't this case study you're griping about have to be done?" Saundra asked between spoonfuls.

Bernie agreed that it did.

"You know, sometimes the teachers at my school are such butts. They get their wires crossed and I have five periods of homework on one night! I mean, don't these teachers think we do anything BESIDES school? It's like teachers don't have a life so they try their best to ruin everyone else's so we're as miserable as they are. A couple of times I even had six classes pour it on ..."

Bernie nodded noncommittally.

"I'm not complaining... OK. I *am* complaining, but stay with me, I really have a point ..."

Bernie nodded some more.

"Which I'll get to if you won't interrupt ..."

" ..."

"OK. The only class I don't mind doing the work for is English. Mrs. Hutchinson is a terrific teacher and she always gives cool assignments. So ... I always do her work last. The other stuff has to be done anyway. If I get *it* out of the way then I can focus on what I really *want* to do," Saundra explained and then continued. "So ... do you like my Mom or what?"

Bernie indicated that he did indeed "like" her Mom and the subject turned to music.

The next day, the three of them went shopping in The Grove.[5] Bernie split off and bought Saundra some very nice and moderately expensive gold earrings. They bore the shape of a tiny mermaid dangling on a light chain. Later, when Jane and Saundra left for Ormond, Bernie put his arm on Saundra's shoulder as she was getting in the car and handed them to her. He closed the door and went around to the lady he "liked."

"She's a good kid, Jane." Bernie replied in response Jane's quizzical expression. He kissed her as affectionately as any boyfriend could manage with his girlfriend's daughter looking on, making gagging gestures. They drove off, Jane beet red and Saundra rolling in laughter.

Bernie went back to pace some more at the lab.

Saundra had, of course, been right. He had reached the same conclusion himself weeks ago. The case study had to come first. There was more than enough data accumulated to write it. By refusing to submit to the task, he was demonstrating stubborn pettiness, throwing a passive-aggressive tantrum because he couldn't do exactly what he wanted.

Surrounded by the trappings of his reputation, the laboratory, students who worshipped him, graduate assistants who felt he walked on water, and a very supportive department, Bernie had disguised his pettiness as some noble "pursuit of truth." Had he not been dating Jane Peterson—whom he "liked"—he could have maintained that lie for at least another year. Saundra's blunt observation had instantly vaporized that delusion. Now, embarrassed that a high school kid displayed more wisdom than he was showing, he knew it would be much worse if the weekend arrived and he *still* had nothing to add during their ice cream session.

After over five hundred years and six months, it was long past time for the world to meet Namor.

Bernie retrieved his dinged-up, but reliable and fully charged, laptop. The flat screen glowed as he downed the fourth and last shot of the coffee. Using the screen as a flashlight, he went out to the porch and set up on a rocking chair. He typed slowly but continuously, diverting from his task only to access his files or the internet through the wireless university network. He worked all night and through the early morning. When his assistants came to work, he emailed the document to his proofreader and took the staff out to breakfast. Then he gave them the day off and went home to sleep comfortably for the first time in six months.

CHAPTER
5

Excerpts from Dr. Bernard Sherban's Famous Paper

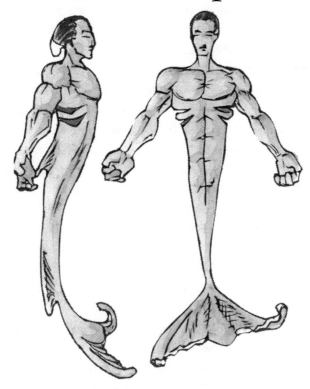

Figure 1: Full Figure reconstruction of Homo Aquaticus: *Front and Side View.*

Analysis of the Anatomy and Physiology of
Homo sapiens sapiens aquaticus

By Dr. Bernard Sherban
University of Miami Biology Department

Abstract:

Unusually high hurricane activity in the months of August and September 2004 partially diverted the flow of the Tomoka River in northeast Florida, exposing a skeleton that, on October 3, 2004, was discovered by a fisherman named Manuel Gomez (see acknowledgments). Several factors such as the positioning of the body (supine, arms folded) and numerous fragments of terran plant and animal remains found in the same rock suggest that the specimen was buried on land that was once a sandy beach. Carbon dating sets the skeleton age at approximately 500 years. The skeleton is complete and very well preserved as a result of the submersion of that gravesite shortly after it was created.

Gender is inconclusive, given the extreme modification of the pelvis,[1] and the absence of soft tissue in the fossilized remains, but the large size (1.87m)[2] and broadness of the shoulders suggest that this was a male. The skeleton has subsequently been nicknamed "Namor" for convenience in referencing. Facial reconstruction reveals a definitive Native American lineage. Had only the upper torso been found, the conclusion would inevitably have been that the remains were of a Timucuan. The Timucua were a tribe of Native Americans indigenous to that region.

It is the determination of this study, however, that although there may be a genetic link to terrestrial humans, this skeleton is not *homo sapiens*[3] *sapiens*,[4] but rather a new subspecies where evolutionary processes have adapted the known human form to an aquatic existence. The proposed name of this subspecies of hominid is *homo sapiens sapiens aquaticus*. Multiple factors in the specimen, most prominently the duel adaptations—convergence of the lower appendages from two legs to one powerful tail, and the transformed thoracic cavity for possibly extracting oxygen from water—support this extraordinary claim and are covered in detail within the body of this paper.

The focus here will be on describing the structure and proposed function of the discovered aquatic adaptations. "Best Guesses" on how those adaptations perform will be offered, but they are preliminary and scrutiny is encouraged. A scenario explaining how Namor came to be will also be proposed, but it, too, is preliminary and offered as a baseline from which future discussion can branch.

The fate of Namor and the remainder of his proposed species, along with the implications of this discovery, holds on our understanding of human evolution will be the subject of another publication.

Overview:

Subject:	"Namor." Fossilized human skeleton adapted to an aquatic, and probable marine environment.
Species:	*Homo sapiens sapiens aquaticus* Abbreviated to *Homo aquaticus*
Fossil Age:	Carbon-14 Dating[5] sets burial time at approximately 510 years
Age at Death:	27-33 years.
Cause of Death:	Blunt trauma to the right temple. Other injuries include an unhealed fractured right ulna, most likely also inflicted at the time of his death.
Gender:	Inconclusive, but the data leans towards male.
Length:	1.87m from apex of head to base of tail.

Weight: Estimated at 100-110 kg[6]

Coloration: Unknown, but projected to match tones of
                     Native Americans of the region.

Head:

With very few exceptions, the skull is anatomically identical to *Homo sapiens sapiens* (see Figure 2). A large brain case, flat forehead, and recessed jaw are all indicative characteristics that this is indeed a member of that species. More specifically, facial reconstruction[7] strongly suggests a Native American origin. The skull is intact, and shows no signs of malnutrition or disease other than an unhealed fracture from what must have been a blunt fatal blow administered to the right temple.

The teeth are complete and in impressively good condition, bearing none of the usual cavities and abscesses typical of finds from this time period. All permanent teeth have grown in, which was one of the significant factors in the estimation of age. Several minute nicks on the enamel detected under a scanning microscope provide a clue for the superior dental condition. Namor may have brushed his teeth regularly with a semi-soft object such as a small branch. Similar markings were quite easily reproduced using an oak twig and some cadaver teeth. Another complementary explanation supports the premise that Namor was a marine water breather. The bacteria usually associated with plaque and eventually tooth decay could not survive the highly saline conditions of an organism whose mouth was constantly flushed with salt water.

The skull is uncharacteristically symmetrical, and although not pronounced, the bridge of the nose is sloped uniquely downward. Namor bore an unusually slender nose. It is not so pronounced that it could not fall within normal explanations, but in light of the uniqueness of this specimen, another explanation is warranted. The steep slope may have stretched the nostrils to a more slit-like shape. Through slight rearrangements of the musculature that allows the human nose to crinkle and stretch, he may have had the capacity to seal them. Blocking off the nostrils

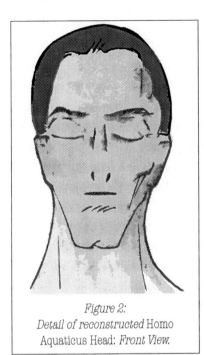

Figure 2:
Detail of reconstructed Homo
Aquaticus Head: *Front View.*

would protect the delicate nasal passages from the abrasion of fast flowing salt water. Namor could then swim at high speeds with his mouth wide open (see behavior) without fear of damage.

Thoracic Region:

At first glance, Namor's ribcage appears undifferentiated. Further study reveals very interesting possibilities. The ribs are inordinately muscled, particularly at the attached ribs'[8] intercostals[9]—almost three times the amount expected for a frame this size. It is conceivable that the extra musculature was necessary to pump the denser medium of water. While not conclusive, this is yet another incidental piece of evidence supporting the possibility that *Homo aquaticus* may have been a water breather. Additionally, there is a hyper-extension of the floating ribs. Their angle of extension from the vertebrae is unparallel to the attached, forming a significantly wider gap between these last two pairs of bones than in the first ten. Further inspection reveals that in stark contrast to their attached counterparts, these ribs are completely devoid of any sort of musculature and show significant weathering of the edges. Several plausible explanations of the duel anomalies exist, but the most comprehensive supposition implies the presence of a pair of slits in the lower thoracic cavity, thus improving breathing efficiency by providing one way fluid flow.

Abdominal Region:

The pelvis is essentially gone, having evolved into a 25th vertebra. The buoyancy of the environment and thick abdominal muscles must have taken the role of lending support to the organs of that region. Having only the skeletal portions available, soft tissue arrangements are difficult to ascertain. Some parallels may be drawn by studying other mammals which have migrated to the waters—particularly dolphins and seals. Namor however presents a new circumstance. If the working premise proves correct, his ancestors were originally bipeds with a significantly different orientation to start with. It is the assertion of this study that the placement of organs such as the digestive, reproductive and renal systems in Namor would approximate human parallels, but, given the absence of supporting evidence, such a connection would be based purely on conjecture and is therefore tentative and unreliable. While this researcher acknowledges that such conjecture is inevitable, this report is not the appropriate venue to present them.

The spinous process[10] of the lowest lumbar vertebrae[11] protrudes further than what is expected on a human frame. It is longer, narrower, and slanted towards the tail roughly parallel to the much reduced fibulas. While this could be merely an anomaly, again there exists an alternate explanation. Dorsal fins provide tremendous stability in aquatic propulsion,[12] and have evolved in several aquatic mammalian species and most of the two fish classes.[13] Both the processes and fibulas occur in strategically advantageous locations for such extensions. Thus, it is a safe assertion that Namor most likely sported a pair of dorsals.

Arms:

Namor was well muscled, but not inordinately.

His fingers are slightly longer than a typical hand. Some indentations on phalanges[14] do not match up to terrestrial fingers. The deviation is not extreme, and could be merely incidental, or perhaps the merman may have had webbing to facilitate movement through water.

The Tail:

Namor's pelvis has been reduced significantly, and is functionally no more than an expanded vertebra. Both legs have been condensed and fused from the pelvis downward. They are lined up to form a mismatched vertebral column extension similar in function to (although not nearly as efficient as) dolphins and whales. One slightly compacted femur with two protrusions extends from what were the pelvic sockets. Two patellas have been fused and inserted between the femur and tibia, acting as another tail bone, thus dramatically reversing their original function and increasing rather than limiting the flexibility at that joint. One tibia meets the patellas. The fibulas are off the vertebral line and are much smaller and thinner than a terrestrial humans'. They also vary in that they are detached from the ankle, jutting dorsally[15] at approximately the same angle relative to the body as the elongated lumbar spinous process. As was mentioned when describing the abdomen, the best explanation leans to a dorsal fin adaptation for stability during locomotion.

The feet are flattened, the phalanges[16] grossly elongated and extended to form a tail-fluke arrangement. Most of the tarsal and metatarsal[17] bones of both feet have been fused into a hard bony knob between the flukes.

Typical for sea mammals, Namor propelled himself through the water with steady powerful up and down strokes of his tail. Back, abdominal, and leg muscles attached throughout the one limb provided the engine. Virtually every muscle from the ribs down realigned for their new role of swimming.

Namor's tail may have performed other functions besides propulsion. The flukes have many tendon connection points. It had, therefore, maintained much of the dexterity of human toes. Additionally, the knob between the flukes is quite dense and, given the torque on the tail, it could conceivably have been a formidable weapon. Multiple healed impact marks on the ventral[18] side make this a very safe determination.

Origins:

It is quite within the realm of interpretation that Namor was not an aquatic organism. He could have been an abnormality kept alive by Native Americans for any of a myriad of reasons. His physical form resembles the rare but well-documented birth defect, Sirenomelia Sequence, also fittingly known as "Mermaid Syndrome." In this lethal disorder, instructions to assemble the body below the ribs are disrupted resulting in the fusion of the lower limbs and hence a "mermaid" like shape.

Ironically the most prominent manifestation of Mermaid Syndrome—the fused legs—in itself is not fatal. In all but two cases[19] however, additional errors in the assembly of the adjoining organs such as kidneys and the digestive tract were too extensive for medical intervention to succeed. The cause of Sirenomelia is unknown. Its frequency is estimated to be in the order of approximately one out of every 100,000 births. These sixteen to twenty thousand cases, many having been chronicled in various medical journals, have yet to reveal a preventative treatment.

One of the less extreme Mermaid Syndrome manifestations—dipus—maintains both feet in an orientation similar to that of a sea lion's back flippers and Namor's flukes. The birth of a child with this variation of the Sirenomelia disfigurement, but not its lethal internal complications, is conceivable.

The appearance of a child with Mermaid Syndrome, born into a primitive culture which relied heavily on the local waters for sustenance, could easily have led its members to some wild and unpredictable conclusions. Tribal leaders might look for a supernatural explanation and might conclude that this wild and unpredictable occurrence was anything from a gift of the gods, to a manifestation of a god itself, to an omen of evil. Significant birth defects inordinately taxed tribe resources and historically, for the benefit of the group, they were killed immediately. But what if they chose another path? What if a group encountered a defective child, but elected to keep it alive? Namor's appearance could be that of a Mermaid Syndrome child nurtured to adulthood. Occam's Razor[20] in fact initially leads an observer to reach this conclusion.

Deeper analysis of the facts however actually leans Occam strongly towards supporting the notion that Namor was indeed an aquatic organism. The most compelling counterargument is that a Mermaid Syndrome child would be an invalid, requiring constant care. Namor was heavily muscled. His bones showed the stress of a lifetime of vigorous activity. Additionally, the other adaptations (ribs, fingers, nose, etc...) are not random. Each is a modification of the terrestrial human form best explained as a conversion to living underwater. Together they fit a model that is too elegant in its form and functionality to write off as a series of random mutations. The evidence therefore supports the more fantastic claim.

Perhaps Mermaid Syndrome was the original alteration which branched Namor's species off from *homo sapiens sapiens*. Lacking another specimen, or genetic material to study, a determination cannot be made.

A more detailed origination scenario will be proposed at the conclusion of this report, but without significant supporting data, the premise is tentative and does not merit mention within the body of a scientific text.

Physical Appearance:

Namor would have resembled a tall, muscular Native American down to his ribs. His skeletal structure is quite similar to the descriptions of a tribe the Spaniards encountered when they traveled through the region of Florida in the 1500's called the Timucuans. The relics of Nocoroco—a rather large village of this tribe—is in fact within a short walk of Namor's grave, supporting the hypothesis that he originated from them. Timucuan coloration was similar to other Native Americans. Timucuan men wore their hair long and in a knot, and they favored heavily tattooing their bodies. Namor most likely had some interactions with this tribe since he was buried on their land and no records of other humans exist in this region. How much of the Timucuan culture he mimicked is uncertain.

On a side note: Namor's burial was unusual for the Timucuan. Nocoroco burials were done quite fastidiously. The dead were kept in special huts and allowed to rot. Caretakers managed the decay until only the bones remained. These were then transferred to mounds *above* the ground. Namor was clearly buried and very soon after his death. No explanation for this variance is offered, but it is unique enough to mention.

Without a pelvis, Namor's body would appear top heavy, and even more muscular by contrast. His physique however would not have been lean. A layer of fatty tissue would be necessary to avoid hypothermia.[21] Replenishing lost heat and movement through the dense medium of water would keep the build-up from creating large stores.

Namor would have fat, but he would never *be* fat.

Three exceptions distinguishing Namor's upper torso from the terrestrial form are the nose, hands and rib slits.

Namor's nose is quite narrow. It is unpronounced and, unless there is a concerted effort to inspect this feature, or an observer is extremely close up, the narrowness would go unnoticed. The narrowness stretches the nostrils out of their rounded shape, forming a more slit-like arrangement. Given the attachment points of human facial musculature, crinkling and uncrinkling the nose may have had the effect of sealing and unsealing the nostrils.

The hands are proportionally larger than expected (see Figure 3). There is evidence of lateral stress on the hand. Webbing of some sort may have existed between the fingers. How much is inconclusive.

A pair of matching slits between the floating ribs, extending from the vertebrae to the sternum,[22] is likely. Since the cartilage that would have attached them did not preserve, a conclusive statement is unattainable. Sufficient circumstantial evidence does

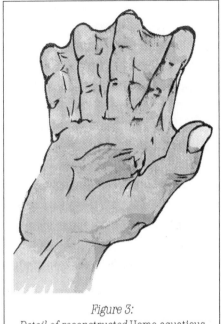

Figure 3:
Detail of reconstructed Homo aquaticus
hand with webbing.

exist to comfortably defend this deduction. These four ribs were firmly connected to the spine, but their angle of extension was unparallel to the ten attached sets. There is no evidence of intercostal musculature; moreover, the bone is worn smoothly where one would expect to find such markings.

These proposed slits represent an intriguing possibility. It is the qualified conclusion of this study that Namor may have surpassed other mammalian migrations from land back to the sea. He may have accomplished the one transition that dolphins, seals, whales, and manatees, could not. Rather than having to surface, Namor may have derived his oxygen directly from the waters of his environment.[23] Slits would be useful in providing an exit point for the water bilging through what would be gills instead of lungs. The observed weathering of the floating ribs is an expected characteristic of material exposed to a lifetime's flow of rapidly pumped sea water. Moving water in and out of the thoracic cavity is twice as efficient if there is an exit point different from the entry. The larger than normal thoracic chamber would also be useful for maximizing the oxygen extraction, as would the sinewy intercostals and diaphragm muscles he apparently wielded. Despite these adaptations, the relative scarcity of dissolved O_2 in even highly oxygenated waters[24] would still be daunting. At the minimum, Namor's breathing would need to be much more rapid than a human of his comparable stature. Whatever organ or organs replaced the lungs must also be significantly more efficient at extracting the O_2. Other behavioral adaptations could also relieve some of the deficiency. When swimming at high speeds for example, Namor perhaps supplemented his bilging by mimicking the strategy employed by sharks—moving with his mouth wide open and his nostril slits shut tight. Secondary studies at various institutes are working out the dynamics of his swim stroke and oxygen capacity, along with the fluid flow through the mouth, and thoracic slits. Their results are eagerly awaited, but it is unlikely their findings will fully account for the oxygen requirements. Barring the discovery of a living representative of Namor's species, the cocktail of adaptations which made the transition possible may never be known.

The lack of complete evidence does not however negate the premise:

Namor was a water breather.

The tail is a marvelous adaptation (See Figure 3). From a propulsion standpoint, successful mammalian adaptations from terrestrial to aquatic environments took on two forms. Both reshaped the role of their hind limbs to create a single powerful segmented appendage with a broad tip to displace as much water as the musculature could manage.

In the case of dolphins and whales, the hind legs all but disappeared and the "push" came from musculature tugging on the vertebrae. The flukes are cartilaginous, forming from an expansion of the tail tip.

In seals and sea lions, the vertebrae musculature does indeed "push," but it was the hind limbs themselves that adapted. The flukes formed from the terrestrial paws and are therefore heavily boned.

Namor seems to have melded a combination of these two techniques. His flukes are most definitively altered feet, but his tail also appears to be in the midst of a long-term metamorphosis. It seems that Namor's species (if he is indeed not unique) is in a transitional phase where the bones of the legs are evolving

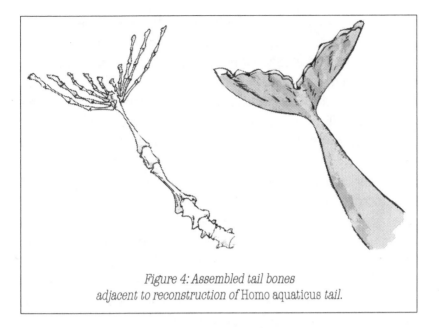

Figure 4: Assembled tail bones
adjacent to reconstruction of Homo aquaticus *tail.*

into three additional vertebrae. The pelvis has all but completed the change. Unfortunately, only if other specimens are unearthed will the accuracy of this supposition be known.

The bony knot at the base may have served as a bludgeoning weapon and hence is addressed as the "ankle club." It was probably thickly calloused from a lifetime of heavy usage resulting in a more leathery appearance. The flukes apparently retained the dexterity of the toes from which they were adapted. Given the tendon attachments, they would have the capability to perform many functions. They could be fanned and retracted much like a peacock's tail. Namor may have employed this versatility for a more efficient swim stroke, or he may have collapsed his flukes to reduce drag if he chose to coast along a current, or leap out of the water.

The presence of digit opposition[25] also suggests that Namor could wrap his flukes around an object. Two possible uses for this would be to lift heavy things with his tail, and the more utilitarian function of allowing Namor to resist the water's currents by anchoring himself to an immobile object such as a reef or rock.

Inspection of the tips of what used to be toes reveals yet another interesting adaptation. Each toe's nail has narrowed and spread to provide a continuous line across the outer edge of the flukes. Having a constantly replenishing tail tip would minimize the inevitable nicks maneuvering through underwater geography would inflict. The sharp edge of the tail would add another dimension to the already formidable weapon that is the ankle club.

Absence of preserved soft tissue means that very little direct evidence on Namor's senses is available. He bears the same skull openings as *homo sapiens sapiens* so it is likely he had the full complement—sight, sound, smell, taste, and touch. In an aquatic environment, the prioritization must have been reworked. Namor's vision would not be as useful, but sound and smell would. And since a marine environment is, by definition perpetually salty, not much use for taste can be speculated. Given the fantastic adaptations he has undergone, it is a reasonable assumption to suggest that a sensory change has also taken place.

Behavior:

Namor moved at great speed and with tremendous maneuverability through his environment by pumping his powerful tail for propulsion and utilizing his arms with possibly webbed hands for maneuvering (see Figure 4). As suggested by the analysis of the head and thorax, he may have been adapted to removing oxygen from the water. If the anatomical supposition is accurate, Namor more than likely swam with his mouth open, bilging water in great volumes through a gill-like organ where lungs would otherwise be. At rest, if his physiological needs were anywhere near parallel to a terrestrial male of comparable size, he must have been a rapid breather. One interesting application of the rib slits is to allow Namor brief visits above water. If he kept his mouth and nostrils shut, Namor could raise his head and arms into the air for brief spells. The bilging would move water in and out of the submerged slits.

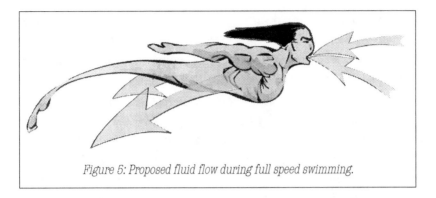

Figure 5: Proposed fluid flow during full speed swimming.

Namor's speed and metabolic requirements categorize him as a likely predator. A diet heavily concentrated in the caloric bounty of fats and oils is the best estimate. Obviously, he ate his food without heating it, but some sort of food preparation must have taken place because his teeth were exceptionally well maintained. There is in fact evidence that Namor "brushed" his teeth. Scanning microscopic analysis of his enamel revealed many uniform microscopic scratches. While such scratches are possible from ingesting hard foods, their evenness suggests that either he ate an extremely consistent diet, or the scratches came from something besides eating. The idea was put forth that perhaps he utilized a tool to clean his mouth and was tested. A small branch from a live oak removed from a tree near the gravesite was taken to the University of Miami Medical School Anatomy Class and, with the permission of the instructor, a cadaver's teeth were cleaned with it, producing similar scratches.

How Namor slept is the subject of two opposing opinions. One notion—torpor[26]—aligns him with other sea mammals. This is unlikely given the complexity of his brain. Namor probably found or constructed some sort of cave shelter and slept anchored by his tail. More study is necessary before either can be ruled out.

To protect himself, Namor wielded a powerful tail loaded at the end with a bludgeon and a razor sharp blade. His "ankle club" would be capable of crushing the skull of an alligator, or knocking a shark aside. The nail along his flukes could slice through several centimeters of flesh. His upper body was also strong enough to inflict harm. Namor's greatest weapon however, would have been his mind. He was intelligent, with a mental capacity no different than contemporary men and women. To reach the age he attained with so little damage demonstrates a hugely successful existence. What tools and tricks he acquired to reach this age may unfortunately never be known. That he came up with them is all but certain. Like many sea mammals, eating and sleeping only took up a fraction of the day. The remainder would have been leisure. It is difficult to fathom what an advanced mind with idle time in such a vast environment would partake in. But it would partake.

Conclusions:

Namor was not only extremely well adapted to his environment. He was also approximately thirty years old and in pristine health when he was apparently murdered. It is difficult to conclude this specimen is an anomaly. In light of this discovery, the anecdotal accounts of sailors throughout written history must be taken more seriously, as should the abundance of references to mermaids and other water folk in our mythos. When all the evidence is objectively considered, fantastic though it may be, the logical conclusion must be that Namor is not a unique organism. Rather, he is the first tangible proof verifying the existence of a distinct and until now unknown species of human which diverged from its terrestrial origins many thousands of years ago.

Conjecture on how this species came to be, as well as how it has remained hidden from the world for so long, is inevitable. Amazing discoveries demand explanations. If none is offered, the vacuum of knowledge will be filled by tabloids and news outlets more interested in splash page headlines and sound bites than the truth. Rather than dooming further studies into denouncing the flurry of wild, uneducated notions, a proactive approach will be engaged. It is with extreme trepidation that this is undertaken. A scientific study is not typically the proper venue to present conjecture unless there is strong data to support the claims. The remarkableness of the circumstances unfortunately has forced an exception. What follows therefore is a proposed "best guess" of how the divergence from a terrestrial habitat occurred. Many of the assumptions necessary to develop this hypothesis are unverified. It is presented solely as a foundation to build from. Over the next several years, now that the existence of *homo aquaticus* is known, it is anticipated that more finds will be made and, as is the case with all science, the working hypothesis will be reevaluated.

###

The "guess" begins with a modest-sized closed population[27] of humans with the distinction that its members carried in their genetic portfolio a pair of remarkable characteristics—the propensity for birthing a non-lethal version of Sirenomelia Sequence and a mutation, which has not been documented, that considerably altered the lungs. Outside the hypothetical realm, there is no real evidence of the existence of this second anomaly, so it was not mentioned in the body of this study. It is certainly a possibility that Namor could have been an aquatic air breather. No other explanation however fully accounts for the extra thoracic musculature, the wide expanse between the floating ribs or the nasal slits. Additionally, a water breather need never surface, which goes far to explain their ability to have remained hidden from verifiable human observation.

As to how this fantastic transformation of lungs to gills occurred, perhaps there was a mutation shutting down the genes responsible for assembling the lungs. Then in the void, a historically dormant section of DNA, which produced gills, was instead activated. Much of the human genome is comprised of these redundant and dormant sequences called "psuedogenes,"[28] passed on faithfully without expression like illiterate monks transcribing bibles. In this way, living things carry the remnants of all the species from which they have evolved. While it is unusual for a gene to pull a trait from such a distant ancestor, it is not outside the realm of possibility. The anomaly could also have been created from completely novel adaptation, as of yet unchronicled by science. The specifics of the engine responsible for the metamorphosis are not important for this hypothetical scenario, only the acceptance that they existed.

The final requirement would be that the population lived and worked close to the water. Typically, tribes in an aquatic environment divided the labor by genders. Men would venture inland to hunt. The women, in turn, would have spent a considerable portion of their time along the shore gathering food, fishing, tending nets, etc. It follows, then, that a disproportionately large number of births would inevitably occur there.

The first successful *homo aquaticus* was likely produced when a woman from this group working near the water collapsed into labor. Tended by the others around her, she would have given birth to an infant bearing both the *Sirenomelia* and the lung transformation traits. The physical appearance of this child must have horrified the witnesses. Monstrously deformed, the grotesqueness of the appearance greatly amplified as it writhed with the torment of asphyxiation. The sounds and color change may have invoked deeper revulsion or perhaps pity. In either case, in this close proximity to water, a decision to drown the dying creature rather than have it suffer appears plausible.

Submerging the child, however, had the opposite effect they anticipated. Rather than dying, when introduced to its life-giving medium, it resuscitated. At this point, without the benefit of modern science, the women would have no explanation for the birth other than the supernatural. Perhaps they considered a baby that breathed water a gift from a god, or a manifestation of god itself. Perhaps they were simply relieved that a child of their group was no longer dying. Infant mortality is notoriously high in populations such as this, all the more so because they carried these duel transformations. It is conceivable that some of them had suffered similar births in their past, but those had never been introduced to the water. They had simply perished from lack of oxygen. If true, the torment of those who had birthed similar children, but had not made the connection with water, must have been excruciating.

It is most likely their pain, stoked by the apparent miracle they witnessed, that motivated their decision to raise the infant. In the water, it would be alive but still helpless. The mother alone could never provide all the resources it would need. A concerted effort must have been necessary. This was probably done in secret without the consent of the group's men.

Normal childbirth in most primitive cultures was traditionally the exclusive realm of the women. Abnormalities would have presented the risk of a volatile response from the males. Rather than assist, they may have elected to kill the infant, declaring it a curse or demon. Even if they initially approved, the first water breather would have been vulnerable for many years, an easy scapegoat for any catastrophe. It would not have survived their wrath beyond a strong storm, large animal attack, bad crop, or poor hunting season. The mere existence of Namor indicates that it did, and since it would likely be otherwise had the males been involved, it is more probable they were kept ignorant in this matter.

With the guidance of the women, the first water breather would learn how to move about using its tail, and to sustain itself in its environment. It would reach adulthood. More births must have occurred over time, with higher chances for survivorship since the women knew the secret of the water, and had inevitably picked up a few tricks from successfully raising the first. Eventually, a sufficient number joined the first to create a reproductively viable population in the waters. It is even conceivable that the water group, being better suited for the task, would have taken over the raising of children born with this pair of anomalies. For future births, women would be encouraged, possibly by the introduction of a ritual, to go for the shore when labor pangs hit in case their child bore the traits that sent them to the water. From the water, the *Homo aquaticus* tribe would wait and watch. If the child was born with lungs and legs, they'd swim off. If it was to go to them, they would gather it.

Meanwhile, in the waters, a new population, not quite closed because of the occasional introductions from the land would, in the absence of any true competition, flourish. The size of this water tribe is open to discussion, but it should have sustained sufficiently large numbers to avoid the complications inherent of small breeding groups. Evolutionary processes would favor those who swam faster and were most efficient in pulling oxygen from the water.

Namor, for example, is too well adapted to have been an initial "gift" to the water. He is definitely a multi-generational product of selective reproduction. Rough estimates indicate that a minimum of fifty to one hundred generations would have been required to chisel Namor's refined form from the initial mold.

Contact with the water and the land would dwindle over time. The principle reason for this was probably that this water group found better habitats. The open ocean is less vulnerable to weather extremes, offers a myriad of resources and, of dire importance, its waters are more oxygenated than inlets. There was also the land group's volatile life. Raids from various tribes throughout all of the Americas were common. Entire groups were taken and absorbed. The introduction of Europeans, both missionaries and conquistadores also decimated small Native American groups. It is probably not coincidental that Namor's death coincided within a few decades of the first Spanish missions.

The best estimate for where this group of humans first lived is near the mouth of the Tomoka River just north of Daytona Beach, Florida. Namor was uncovered there and his upper body features closely resemble the natives from that area as described by the Spanish missionaries. Around that same time, a Timucuan village—Nocoroco—was flourishing close by. The Spanish presence focused on Nocoroco, and they kept excellent records of this and many other missions throughout the time they held a claim to Florida. Nowhere in their literature, not even when describing the pagan customs of the natives, is there a mention of aquatic humans. The loosely organized French traders and military, also wandering through the state in that day, did not record anywhere near as meticulously as the priests, but their scant records are also devoid of aquatic human references. And, the European presence only grew.

The likely explanation is that one of the many ambitious Timucuan kings expanded their reign into this region, annihilating the indigenous population which was producing aquatic humans. Namor's strong Timucuan resemblance suggests that the people were probably Timucuan themselves; a small faction that had broken off from the main Timucuan Tribe living undisturbed until the king's ambitions destroyed them. They could also have been assimilated into Nocoroco. The massive infusion of genetic variety into the population would have been nearly as effective in eliminating the production of water breathers as a slaughter.

Then the Spanish arrived and, through ruthless enslavement and the spread of European diseases, killed the Timucuans, leaving two degrees of separation.

After tyrannical kings and zealous, disease-carrying missionaries wiped out Namor's land ancestors, the encroaching civilization performed the equivalent of "salting the earth." The foundations for many of Florida's modern roads were built of crushed shell and limestone. Unfortunately, the most handily available source for this material were the large shell mounds Florida Tribes created with their spent sea food meals. Hundreds of these archeological wonders were leveled to create a hard, porous bed for the asphalt, obliterating all their secrets. Tribes used the mounds as trash heaps and burial sites. They eventually built their huts on them because, after several years, they became the high ground on this very flat state. It is a disturbing thought to consider how many other clues to Namor's origins tourists are currently driving over on their way to the beaches and theme parks.

On a more whimsical note, we'll consider the fate of Namor's species. There is a cliché oceanographers enjoy citing whenever they appeal to the general public for funding: "We know more about the surface of the moon than the depths of our own oceans." That fact underscores the possibility of Namor's children inhabiting the seas today. The only argument against this notion is that they have never been observed. That was the same argument against their past existence before Namor vaporized it. It can be safely assumed that no serious attempt to discover intelligent life *under* the sea has ever been undertaken, so it is a looming unknown whether any exists.

There are considerable resources probing the cosmos hoping to find a sign of life. That effort is commendable and should continue. There is now, however, a *second* front on which to concentrate: a region which, unlike space, does not depend on cosmic immensity to engender speculation about its secrets. The premise that intelligent life exists elsewhere in the universe is based on the argument that the cosmos is so vast, it *must* hold alternate and/or intelligent life forms. Under the seas however, evidence of intelligence claims no such ambiguity. It has been found. We named him Namor.

If sufficient resources are invested, answers will most certainly emerge. Whether this takes the form of additional archeological artifacts, chronicling the demise of *Homo aquaticus* or, hopefully, a reunion with our living, swimming distant human cousins, remains to be seen.

One final word of caution: Namor's descendants, if they currently survive, must be aware of us. Yet, they have eluded detection for hundreds of years. Assuming that they would want to change this arrangement merely because we now know of their existence borders on absurdity. It is an obvious conclusion that they do not wish to be disturbed. Before we allow our curiosity to overpower civility and set out to disregard their privacy, a concerted effort to discover what made them hide from us in the first place must be undertaken.

It is the strongest supposition of this study and the direction of the next that the answers to *homo aquaticus'* disappearance are hidden somewhere in the chronicles of the early 1500's, particularly those dealing with the New World. Until the cause of their erasure from our awareness is known, the conditions necessary for their return will be a mystery. Attempts to bypass this question and blunder forward will most likely fail miserably, and our civilization may find itself at odds with a sovereign realm … again. This realm's inhabitants however hold a serious home field advantage.

CHAPTER
6

Saundra

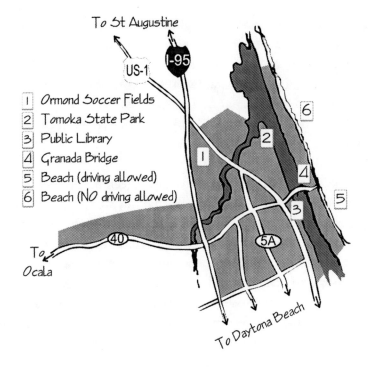

To St Augustine

US-1

I-95

1 Ormond Soccer Fields
2 Tomoka State Park
3 Public Library
4 Granada Bridge
5 Beach (driving allowed)
6 Beach (NO driving allowed)

6

2

1

4

5

3

To Ocala

40

5A

To Daytona Beach

Ormond Beach, Florida

"You knew all along and you never said anything?"

For the hundredth time today, Saundra ignored the accusation.

"Saundra, I'm talking to you. I thought we were, like, BEST friends ... This is like the biggest discovery in the world. I mean, Jeez! Your mom was on CNN last night Oh, and tell her she so has to do something about that 'ranger hair style.' I mean, a *ponytail?* On CNN? National TV? Anyway there she is, right in front of the little merboy's grave, with you right next to her, talking about how everything we've ever learned in history class needs to be retaught? And there used to be mermaids in the Halifax River? And the whole world is different than we thought it was ten seconds before we turned to this channel? And you knew all about it LAST YEAR ... And you never said anything? What kind of a friend are you?!"

That did it.

Saundra twisted the wheel sharply, careening her beat up PT Cruiser onto the dirt shoulder. The rapidly aging car was on its third teen driver so it was well-accustomed to flighty commands and took the instantaneous course alteration in stride. Tires grumbled, kicking up loose rocks, adding a few more dings to the already seriously-traumatized wood paneling, as they desperately sought a grip on the loose earth. The tires found their hold, jarring suddenly to a halt, six feet from a "Speed Limit 45" sign. An enormous dust cloud, rooster tailing in the cruiser's wake, overtook them, blocking out what little sunlight remained in the day.

Sitting in the darkened cabin, both still slick and grubby from soccer practice, Saundra contemplated what exactly she had to say for her friend to drop the subject. Nothing she had tried all day seemed to have an effect. But then again, in the decade or so Saundra had known her, she couldn't remember a time Jessica Van Patten ever shut up ... ever!

Jessica's mouth was notorious. In the classroom, teachers dreaded her. She was one of those paradoxical students. She received good grades, but was constantly serving detentions because she simply had to blurt out every thought that crossed her mind, as if *thoughts* had some type of expiration date where they would go "bad." On the soccer field, she was a magnificent forward, but her mouth complicated her performance and instigated as many fights as her leg scored goals.

To be fair, Jessica didn't start any of the fights. Typically, around the third quarter, an opposing player couldn't take it anymore and, in a vain attempt to silence the chatter, slammed into her. Her constant talking was responsible for her very voluminous boyfriend tally. She went through about one per week. Her long, flowing blonde hair, tan, healthy skin, and drop dead gorgeous beach girl looks were irresistible to her male SeaBreeze High School classmates, but her incessant mouth ran them off after a weekend. At the rate she was going, Saundra had estimated that Jessica would date the entire junior class before commencement.

But Jessica didn't see her mouth as a problem. She was certain everyone wanted to talk as much as she did but they were simply too inhibited—a problem that never plagued Jessica.

Much to the dismay of Saundra McFarlane.

Saundra was a bizarre "best friend" choice for Jessica. She was quiet, studious, and completely uninterested in the intricate social workings of a teen life. Yet somehow, without planning it, the two girls seemed to wind up in the same circumstances. They both joined the same competitive soccer league, both chose striker, but wound up as forwards—Jessica right, Saundra left. They competed in writing contests, often alternating first and second places, took the same classes, joined the same Girl Scout troop, and went to the same parties.

They even looked similar. Both wore their hair wavy and long and were about the same height, slender, and athletic. "Lungs with

legs" the coaches would call them. They varied only in their coloration; Saundra's red hair, green eyes and fairer skin to Jessica's Malibu
Barbie tones. It was inevitable that they become friends.

The only real decision they ever split on was their choice of
high school. After middle school, Jessica selected Sea Breeze because it was where most of her friends were going. Saundra chose
Spruce Creek because it offered an IB program.[1] That created a rift
which never really healed. Jessica couldn't understand why Saundra
chose to drive the extra distance to be far from her friends merely to
do extra work and Saundra couldn't fathom why Jessica was such a
butt about her choice.

But Jessica was a butt about every choice that she didn't understand.

Like now ...

With the merman revelation ...

She was a butt ...

A talking butt that wouldn't get over it!

Granted the entire school, and probably the world for that
matter, was humming with the breaking news, but for Saundra, the
news had been "broken" for quite a while. Keeping the secret for a
year was an infuriating burden, but she had done so for her mom's
sake and for Bernie too.

Her father was most definitely furious that she hadn't confided
in him. Three missed calls from his number sat in her cell phone
memory. She didn't plan on returning them. He'll just be angry and
hurt of course, but he was always angry and hurt, especially if it
involved Bernie. The rest of the family would also have a problem,
but Mom could handle them.

Most of her friends didn't mind being shut out. They either
understood why she kept silent, or they didn't care. If anything, the
revelation helped Saundra's classmate relationships. She was aloof half
the time anyway. This actually explained much of her "aloofness."

Her single bright spot was Nathan.

Nathan had been terrific. Saundra had run to his house moments after the press conference interrupted the prime time line-

up. They lived only a few streets apart so she arrived to find him on the phone trying to get through to her house. She and Nathan had been friends since they rode the same bus to elementary school, but they'd only been dating for six months now. When Saundra chose the Spruce Creek IB program, they had lost touch.

Nathan went to Sea Breeze.

They had bumped into one another while walking in the neighborhood late one afternoon. She almost didn't recognize him. The Nathan she remembered was a big-headed, funny looking, skinny kid who never stopped smiling. This Nathan was dashing. Close cropped, short blonde hair, and broad shoulders that had seen their fair share of a weight room, filled out his Tropicana Spring Break T-Shirt. He wore loose fitting, comfortable jeans and white sneakers. She first thought it was some college kid looking for his hotel.

Then he turned and she immediately recognized him. He still had that smile. After catching up on their lives, Nathan walked her home, asked her to go to the movies that weekend, and he kissed her lightly on the cheek but teasingly close to her mouth.

"I've wanted to do that since seventh grade," he said.

"I've been hoping you'd do that since fourth," she replied with a shy smile.

And they'd been dating since. It wasn't an easy relationship. They hardly went anywhere. Soccer practice lasted well into the evening and she was constantly slammed with school work. As for Nathan … Nathan was busy too.

But he was so sympathetic.

"I can't believe you kept that bottled up for an entire year," he told her as he hung up the phone with one hand and swept her into a hug with the other.

"Me?" he continued, "I'd have sung it from the top of the highest building I could find."

And he literally would have too. Nathan was an actor/singer/dancer. He was brilliant. He landed the lead in just about every performance Sea Breeze High School's Arts Academy held, and he did it all with an unassuming casual elegance rarely found among the highly volatile, emotion-soaked theatre creatures. Audiences who experienced one of Nathan's shows left feeling they had witnessed the beginnings of greatness.

That's how he made Saundra feel too. To her, Nathan was in the midst of a lengthy, one man, passion play, exclusively written and performed for her, starring in the role he was born to play— "The Perfect Boyfriend."

Why couldn't Jessica—her BEST friend since kindergarten— be as understanding as a boyfriend of six months?

She had endured Jessica's bombardment from the time her friend read the front page story at Starbucks and then all day at school. She had taken it throughout soccer practice but now, tired, in her own car and doing Jessica a favor by giving her a ride home; she did not choose to take it anymore.

She sucked in deep slow breaths, trying to regain her composure. Jessica breathed heavily too, but for a different reason. She had been trying to get her cleats off when the sudden lurch slid her down the seat. Now her head was even with the arm rest and her feet were nearly vertical. In this awkward position, she could not reach the seatbelt. She was essentially trapped, and in a second they both knew it. Saundra made no move to free her.

"I wasn't *allowed* to tell you Jessica. Mom signed one of those nondisclosure things. If I told *anyone* she'd be in all sorts of legal trouble. Besides, it would have ruined Bernie's work."

"Saundra—"

"And another thing, you can't be trusted with a secret. You talk and talk and talk, and sometimes I don't even think *you're* listening to yourself."

"Saundra—"

"I don't mean you'd purposely tell someone else, but you talk so much Jessica, it'd be bound to slip out."

"Saundra—"

"And then where would our friendship be? I betray the trust of both my mother AND the pretty decent guy she's seeing. They'd be in trouble. I'd be in trouble. *You'd* be in trouble … and for what?"

"Saundra—"

"Should I risk all that? And for what? Just so you can know a secret that I don't think you care much about anyway! Is that it?"

"Saundra—"

"Honestly Jessica, I'm getting so sick of your badgering. I've had a hell of a time keeping it bottled in and I was hoping you'd be more understanding."

"Saundra?"

"No, don't 'Saundra?' me! I think you owe me an apology. I think you've been a jerk to me all day. And I think you have to start learning to shut up or you're going to have to find someone else to harass!"

"*Saundra?*"

"What!"

"I'm really stuck here … OK, you're right. I don't really care all that much about the merman. Science isn't my thing. I was just making conversation … I'm sorry I got carried away. Can you get me loose now … please?"

Saundra unclipped the seat belt. Jessica squirmed to a less horizontal position and picked up her monologue where she left off.

"Thanks," she said, straightening up at last. "Besides, so what if they found the little merboy. I mean it's not like Ariel's brother is frolicking in the oceans just off shore. It was like a thousand million years ago right … Right? And who was that "Mister Gomez" guy? The announcer said an old Mexican man found the skeleton and he tried to say it with a Spanish accent but didn't succeed. Don't you hate it when someone tries too hard to sound like they know another language? And did he really turn down an interview with CNN because he had to go to Chili's for dinner? What's up with that? I mean, can't they go there some other night? I mean *it is* CNN. Am I right? Saundra, am I right?"

Jessica finally took a breath and realized Saundra wasn't paying attention. The two sat quietly in the air conditioning, a CD Nathan burned for Saundra filling the silence. It was old stuff — Sinatra, Martin, Crosby — and a bunch of other crooning dead guys he was hoping Saundra would enjoy.

She did.

They were calm, sophisticated, easy on the ears, and a lot more interesting than the blather streaming from her friend.

Without speaking, Saundra popped the stick into gear, and started out again. She drove mechanically, having taken this route countless times before. Dean Martin crooned "*Amore*" as she traveled along US-1 towards the heart of town, past the industrial complexes outside Ormond Beach. At the Tomoka River Bridge, she felt the churning metal wheels of a northbound train. When she was younger, watching a train cross the river bridge was one of her favorite sights. She would consider it a good luck omen if both the train and the car she was in crossed at the same time. Today, she was merely glad it was going in the opposite direction, and would not block her way when she reached the intersection.

She turned off the broad straight highway through her town, that connected Miami to Maine, maneuvering to the winding tree-lined streets of Jessica's aptly named "The Trails" subdivision, to the soundtrack of Sinatra's "*The Summer Wind*." Neither exchanged a word, even when they arrived at Jessica's house. Saundra didn't shut the engine off or turn her view from the road, relying on the click of the closing door as her cue to peel out.

She drove through Ormond clenched tightly. It wasn't until she crossed the Granada Bridge and was beachside that she decompressed enough to realize she was furious. She had so badly wanted to tell someone the amazing secret she'd to suppress for the past year! And, of course, she'd wanted to tell Jessica. The stress of keeping her oath of silence was enormous, especially with her unrelenting academic demands and athletic schedules.

On top of all that, her Dad was being a supreme jerk. He was insanely jealous that Mom had found someone to be with and it bothered him to no end that Saundra seemed to like Bernie too. He had cancelled two weekend visits on lame excuses and when she called for clarification, he merely responded, "You and that professor guy seem to get along so well — why don't you spend the weekend with him?"

So she did and that made him even angrier.

Now her best friend was upset, her Dad hated her, school still stunk, *and* she felt like garbage! Why? Was it because she acted responsibly? Because she kept her word? Because she didn't gossip like the other pathetic, stereotypical teenagers she was expected to emulate? Because she honored her Mom's request?

Because she didn't hate Bernie?

WHY?

This was so wrong!

Today had been one of the worst days at school ever and it should have been magnificent. She was a celebrity. Bernie was on every network last night, announcing the publication of his findings and answering questions. Afterwards, cameras switched to her Mom on site at the park, describing how Namor's skeleton was secretly transported, and how she and Bernie's assistants had combed the entire park with no positive results. And Saundra was right next to her, a big dopey proud grin etched on her face.

Each class period, her teachers and classmates had grilled her for details. The principal had even come by during second period to say "Hi" ... and to have his picture taken with her. The disruption was so intense, there was hardly any homework tonight.

What's more, Saundra considered herself a naturally cheerful person. Why, then, did she feel so miserable?

She needed to sort through these feelings with someone. Mom would be useless. Most of her solutions centered on a hug and some brownies. Saundra'd enjoy both, but neither would offer answers. Nathan might understand but she was worried she'd sound whiny. Their relationship was too new for this kind of conversation. So, in a logic tangle only a teen mind could unravel, Saundra reasoned that she had to make sure Nathan thought of her as strong before she showed she could be weak as well. Besides, mentioning Mom and Nathan was merely a gesture of courtesy.

Saundra *knew* who she was going to talk to.

Bernie had been so great, almost as awesome as Nathan. Immediately after he'd sent his study off for review, Bernie had begun his quest in ancient literature to uncover the fate of Namor's descendants. He traveled constantly for two months, criss-crossing the world, soliciting relevant fourteenth-century documents from museums and private owners in the United States, Spain, Portugal, Italy, France, England, even Vatican City. Hundreds of translated papers were gathered in UPS and FedEx boxes piled against every wall of his modest Coconut Grove house.

Unpacking had converted the box towers to paper heaps (Bernie refused to work with e-data on the grounds that, "Deleting is too bland. I need to be able to crumple up a useless document." The clutter grew so dangerously large that it spread to the guest house and Saundra and her Mom had no place to stay when they went down.

Not to be denied their company, Bernie started visiting Ormond. At the end of the week, he'd sweep up a nest of promising papers, hop on the interstate, and stay with them in the guest room. He and Jane would go through the piles in between long walks on the beach, and exploring the interesting pockets of communities in the area. Whether it was an art show in New Smyrna Beach, shopping in Deland, a street party in downtown Daytona, a fortune telling in Cassadega, or the Azalea Festival in Palatka, their day always wound down on the couch; Bernie reading and Jane sleeping, her head on Bernie's lap.

Bernie would continue plodding until Saundra came over. It took a few minutes for him to free his thigh. Waking Jane was out of the question, so he engaged in a precise prop replacement, not unlike Indiana Jones replacing the gold skull with a similarly weighted bag of sand. Molding a nearby cushion to match the shape of his thigh, he gently cradled Jane's head with his arm and, in one smooth, well practiced move, slid the cushion in as he freed his leg. He'd kiss Jane tenderly on the cheek and the two night people would head to the kitchen.

Ormond Beach also had Publix ice cream.

Their chats had become the highlight of Saundra's weekend. On the rare Saturdays she and Nathan were free enough to go out, Bernie would wait up. Later, over their new favorite, Crazy Almond

Vanilla, the three of them basked in a conversational free-for-all, debating the ethics of stem cell research, the relevance of Radiohead vs. Pink Floyd, the talents of Steve Martin vs. Adam Sandler, the underlying arguments behind Evolution vs. Creationism, and the gameplay of Asteroids vs. Halo 2.

She was in heaven.

And that was the essence of her dilemma. Her heaven involved two men who did not belong in the life she lived. Both emerged while she was immersed in the conspiracy of keeping Namor secret. Her need to vigilantly guard her "secret" had detached her from many associations she'd been comfortable with since childhood. Bernie obviously came in with the discovery, but she was relatively certain Nathan would never have kissed her that night had she not seemed so disconnected.

Now that the secret was out, her old life was creeping back and Saundra wasn't so sure she wanted it to.

Pulling up to her driveway, Saundra was annoyed initially that there were no spaces left, but her outlook brightened when she recognized the barricade consisted of Bernie's truck and Nathan's million-year-old lime-green (where the paint still clung) Cadillac. Neither was expected. It was only Thursday. Nathan had rehearsal tonight and Bernie's university obligations always held him in Miami until Friday. Yet there they were. Saundra was overwhelmed with the urge to see them. She flew out of her car, haphazardly grabbing the enormous backpack and gym bag she lugged daily. Bits of her life sloughed off the poorly-closed luggage, leaving an eclectic comet trail of jock and nerd paraphernalia. She hurdled the front porch and loudly, sweaty, breathless and disheveled, burst in the room.

"Hi Mom! Bernie! Nathan! Wow, this is great. Cool! Nathan, don't you have rehearsal tonight? What're doing here? Bernie, it's only Thursday, what a surprise! How'd you get away? Bernie? … Nathan? … Mom?"

No one noticed

Bernie and Jane were entrenched on the love seat carefully going over a printout. Nathan was sprawled on the couch. He too held a stack of papers. They all seemed engrossed, and for the most part ignored her. Only Bernie made any gesture. He handed her a stack of twenty sheets of laser-printed computer paper.

"I put a bunch of sodas in the fridge. Grab something to drink and find a comfy spot. There're 204 pages and only one copy. Jane's on 61–80, I'm nearly done with my third reading, and Nathan's on ... what?"

"21–40" Nathan muttered, not breaking his read.

"O.K., so you follow Nathan ... I think I found Namor."

Bernie returned to his pages as soon as Saundra took the sheets. She noticed, on his lap, a nearly full, note-cluttered legal pad where he was recording his thoughts on the mysterious paper. Jane threw Saundra a smile and Nathan bent his knees so she'd have a space on the couch. Other than that, the three most important people in Saundra's life were oblivious to her presence.

Initially she was frustrated at this, especially given the turmoil she was experiencing. But her curiosity over the document in her hands quickly overshadowed her other sentiments.

Popping a Mountain Dew from the selections Bernie had stocked, she plopped next to Nathan. He still wouldn't stop reading, but his hand stretched over and touched hers softly. Saundra took a sip and glanced around the room. She finally relaxed. She was where she belonged. Her friends, the soccer team, schoolwork, even Jessica were wonderful, but they were from another time, and related to another person. These three people reading silently in perfect comfort with one another were her world now.

Saundra wrote a note on her hand to remind herself to call Jessica and apologize for being such a butt and to pick up all the gear she had just littered in the yard. Turning to the papers Bernie handed her, what she originally thought were computer printouts were, in fact, crisp copies of old typewritten pages, each bearing a bluish seal of a crucifix with the words "*La Santa Sede*" encircling it, on the upper right corner. It appeared to be very important. She nudged Nathan's knee until he looked over. Saundra pointed to the seal.

"Vatican City" was all Nathan said before returning to his read.

Saundra wanted to ask Nathan when he had arrived. She wanted to know what made Bernie so certain about this document, and what Mom's impression of the work so far was, but a quick glance to the entranced readers made it clear she was going to get nowhere with any of the three until they finished.

Saundra read the title;

Diary of the False Priest Francisco Sabatez
Created 15 July 1507:
Archived in the Vatican Library 21 November 1511
Transcribed from the original Spanish
on 9 March 1964

With a sip of Mountain Dew, Saundra began her read ...

CHAPTER 7

The Diary of
the False Priest

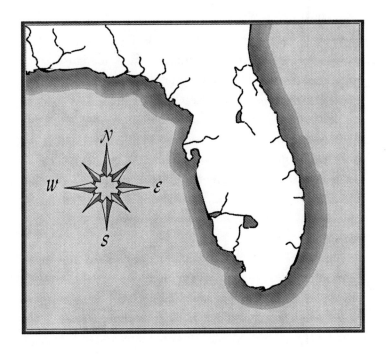

Map of the New World's Southernmost peninsula, 1500.

(Transcriber Note: Although sequentially, this section was placed before the main body of this text, presumably by the author, the ink lightness and the shaky handwriting suggests it was written after the contents of the document were finished.)

Dear reader, I have been adrift for eight days on this tiny vessel. I know I ride a current which will steer me in the path of merchant ships. I know, as well, that any intersection will occur long after I have perished. Most likely, then, you have wrested this journal from the clutches of a dead man. So what you will learn from it is a ghost's tale. Do not fear the lesson. We, the dead, have much to teach.

Please forgive the shaky script you are forced to endure. My hand trembles with the weakness of my thirst. And do not over-chastise the tint, nor the lightness of my prose. My ink has been evaporating nearly as rapidly as my own body's fluids. I can no longer produce sufficient saliva to moisten my quill, and must rely on the blood from a wound on my arm to wet it.

My water has long ago run out, and I had no food to begin with. I fear that my doom is near, and soon I will be judged for my sins in the presence of God. I am certain the verdict will be swift and merciless. It is what I should expect from a just God, for my life's sins are many and unforgivable. I have placed these final thoughts on paper, chronicling the events that transpired which resulted in my current mortal predicament as a final act of penance. Perhaps it will gain me reprieve from the punishing flames …

Perhaps not.

It matters not to me. My fate is irrelevant ...

My message is not.

I beseech you to not discount my words. Read them as a factual record and not the ramblings of a delirious sinner. Take warning and learn from my mistakes. Do not repeat them or my consequences will be yours as well. Know now what I learned unquestioning: that our God is truly miraculous, and tho' his latest miracle has been cast as a tool of vengeance on my person, I cannot hide my wonder of it.

So speaks the eternally damned ghost of the False Priest.

(Begin main body of artifact:)

My name is Francisco Emilio Sabatez DeCarta. As you may have deduced, I am the pirate infamously referred to as the False Priest. A title boding a reputation I have enthusiastically cultivated to my advantage. For a decade I prowled the waters of the Atlantic taking what booty came my way through threat of violence or from unleashing the rage of my guns and crew. The means mattered not to me. Only the gold was of import. And yet this day, alone, starving, desiccated by the relentless sun, I ask ... What good is my gold to me now?

I have squandered my life.

My crew has mutinied. They have taken my crippled vessel along with all my gold to parts unknown. I have been marooned on this puny craft with a small skin of rancid rainwater, long gone, as my sole provision. Only the echoes of their fear of me spared my throat from their blades. Or given my suffering, perhaps they feared me not at all and wished me to wither slowly in these wretched waters. Aye, most assuredly the blade would have been more merciful.

I hold no soul but my own to blame for my demise. If my zeal for riches had not overpowered my judgment, I am certain I would still captain my ship this day. I was however approached by a Duke of the Spanish Coast, a harsh ruthless man, who enticed me into this fatal folly. He sought slaves for his fields. Those who were his property did not linger long on this earth and he was constantly replenishing his stocks. After the Spanish purged the Iberian peninsula of the Moor, this Duke had commissioned several slave raids on the Moroccan coast. But Africa was crowding with slavers and the natives were becoming more wary of their approach. Costs were rising and slavers were uniting to fix their prices quite steeply. He sought a less expensive source for his laborers. The stories of sinewy natives in the New World attracted his attention. The Duke sent his minions to the inns where my sort congregated, spreading gold and the hint of much more for the right person to perform the right task. I robbed one, intending to skewer the soft pudgy courtier, lest he live on to add to the already hefty bounty on my head, but he spoke quickly and desperately. His message delivered, I sent him back to his lord with a reply;

"Speak on. The False Priest is listening."

Through intermediaries, I discussed his want and my bounty for acquiring it. He required a steady delivery of slaves and I faced the pirate's paradox; my goodly share of gold but a hefty price on my neck kept me from the pleasures of spending it freely. Through many nights our emissaries rode to and fro negotiating a mutually satisfactory arrangement. In the end, I would exploit my knowledge of the seas and establish a private, clandestine slave chain consisting of three ships delivering a cargo of laborers every four months.

In return, I would be a Baron. A full ten percent of his lands would he cede to me, and ten percent of the delivered slaves from the routes to work them. My crimes would be exonerated in gratitude for the service I had done my Duke. And I could burn this wretched priest garb and live out my years in luxury.

It was an evil contract sealed by two evil men, and I rue the day I conceded to the terms.

Before, however, I was unrepentant. Was I not the bold False Priest? Did I not scorn the church itself by donning the garb of its representative? Truly, my very colors bore the most sacred crucifix beside the skull and bones. I held no fear of man or god. And I was determined to be a rich man.

But I was not stupid. Vast though the oceans may be, as a pirate I knew they would not conceal routes forever. And a slave ship laden with cargo was incapable of outrunning or outfighting a warship. I could therefore not exploit the islands Spain colonized after that imbecile Columbus stumbled upon them. The natives had been slaughtered for the most part and those who remained were either enslaved to work or hiding in numbers too few to bother with.

But the imbecile stopped short of the true New World. He was so content to discover *anything* that Columbus settled for a fistful of sparse islands when an entire continent lay just beyond. And even those tiny islands were snatched from him by the more ruthless elements of the king's court. He perished a bitter failure, all his work stolen. And of the continent, the fool never knew.

A pirate however must make use of all available resources. Many a scurrilous crew had been aware of the great land north of Cuba and Hispaniola, teeming with tall, robust natives who could survive an arduous journey in a hold and still contribute many years of sweat in our fields. Eventually the Spanish would reach this land, but I would be long buried, a very fat content Baron, out of the reach of Spanish justice.

My exploits had been thwarted of late, an unfortunate hazard of notoriety. The very fear my colors struck on my victims stoked the embers of ambition within my pursuers.

With visions of promotion swirling in their heads, I was re-
peatedly attacked where a more clear-minded captain would
not dare. As always, I prevailed, downing those who so eagerly
wished to be sunk. Their failures enhanced my reputation,
but I suffered a series of minor losses to my vessel, diminish-
ing my crew's numbers to the point that I needed replace-
ments. I demanded of the Duke a crew of Portuguese for the
undertaking. There is no finer sailor in all the world and I
desired reliable comrades for the voyage, but he would not
open his coffers sufficiently. Instead I was forced to sign on a
mangy cast of Spanish cutthroats, a third of whom remained
sequestered until we were well at sea.

I charted a course well north of the established routes,
thus avoiding even the most errant of ships. Weather and winds
favored my journey and the coast of my destination was sited
in only two months time. A brief hunting venture ashore to
replenish water and meat also yielded the first cargo. A small
group of natives, perhaps a family, were captured. A few escaped into the bog and my barbarians mishandled some who
would otherwise have survived.

After all was done and the smoke cleared of the muskets,
the rain barrels were filled, the aroma of fresh meat swirled
from the stewpot, and five slaves lay in shackles below. They
were not giants, but the two men and three women towered
over my crew by many inches. They were certainly a prize
greater than the black-skinned stock supplied by the Moors. I
confess that a glee overcame me. If all we captured were of this
quality, my success was ensured. My ship had fresh supplies
and quick success. I was emboldened.

I set sail on a northward trek, tracing the coastline. This
expedition's imperative was not merely the acquisition of slaves,
but the establishment of an outpost where slaves might be
gathered for processing. I intended to maroon the sequestered
men at the outpost and trade them goods for cargo every four
months time.

A further vindication of the brilliance of my plan came as I observed the abundance of natives along the shore. The land teemed with those who I would have toil my fields. Word of our aggressive motives must have been passed along by those who escaped. From the ship we witnessed large masses of the native populace taking flight inland upon setting eyes on our sails. Their communication outpaced our progress and soon we saw naught of the natives. But they were unquestionably there. In their haste to vanish from us, they neglected to conceal the materials of their daily lives. While no living native was visible, huts, fishing nets and the large hollow trees they used as boats plainly revealed their presence.

For reasons I do not particularly fathom, I declined many a promising harbor. Perhaps it was my desire to place a wealth of water between my outpost and the Spanish colonies; perhaps I sought a sign; perhaps my greed sought a great accumulation of natives. Perhaps it was God maneuvering me to my doom. Finally, in four days, I found my destination. An enormous gaping river mouth broke the coastline. Not very far inland, extending along both shores of its banks, the smoke of many village fires made known a plentiful supply of slaves.

Indeed, there were thousands. And these natives did not run.

Quite the contrary.

My spotter heralded an armada of the tree boats, laden with four spear-wielding men apiece, approaching with malice. Eyeing my attackers with a spyglass, my first impression was that they were quite heavily garbed for the tropical climate. Closer scrutiny, however, revealed they were as scantily clad as I expected savages in warm clines to be. They had simply adorned their bodies, from face to feet, with intricate colorful markings that appeared permanent. I had seen body markings before. They were common among seafarers, adorning even this unworthy crew, but never had I witnessed such an extreme application. It was quite grotesque, as if they painted on their clothing.

I laughed aloud, heartily and with arrogance, at the folly of their attack. We were armed with the most modern weaponry: metal armor, strong muskets, and cannons on all sides. They wielded naught but sticks with a sharpened rock at the tip.

But their numbers were staggering!

The armada would not cease to spill from the river. Into the hundreds it grew, with no end to them perceivable. I ordered the ship about and retreated to their South.

I did not fear them. Truly, God had not divined his vengeance yet and, barring that revelation, I feared nothing. I merely saw no logic in setting cannons on natives I needed alive. A slave cannot work my fields if he has been torn asunder. Let the colorful creatures believe they had frightened us off. They would soon know otherwise. They would soon know true fear.

Tacking South for a day, I discovered an inlet leading to a safe harbor nestled between a barrier island and another, more modest river mouth. Wind and tide were with me and, in moments, I was anchored and feeling quite secure. The geography was ideal. Deep water for my ship, soft sloping sand for quick disembarking, potable water, lumber and game a plenty.

It was my intent, now, to claim *this* location as the site for my outpost. Here, not much more than five days' walk from the great collection of natives, I would build my fortifications undisturbed. Once the walls were erected, the slaves could be harvested through raids. Eventually, as in Africa, I was confident the natives themselves would learn the futility of resistance, and their chieftains would deliver us our quota in return for a trifle and the assurances that they would otherwise be left alone. I announced my vision to the cheers of the crew. Too many of the dogs were not of the sea and viewed any landfall as desirable. I doubled the rum rations and that evening, my crew and I slept soundly in the delusion our fortunes were assured.

How foolish I was to have believed such a lie.

Folly all the more painful in the light of what transpired. Had I not chosen that wretched cove as my sanctuary; had I simply attacked the colorful brutes who challenged me on floating trees ...

But I see now that it was God's hand, not my own, that steered the vessel true to my fate. It was He who desired this site, for here it was that the spirits of the sea were in greatest commune with we who are confined to the surface.

In the morrow, a shabby, hungover lot manned the lifeboats and launched to shore. I remained aboard with a skeleton of a crew, annotating my maps. The sodden duties of physical labor were not my responsibility and, having no intent to occupy the outpost, I had no opinion on its design; merely that it reliably produce my wants. In a few short days, a pair of couriers returned aboard with excited news. The construction proceeded apace.

Moreover, they had captured a large number of slaves. The ignorant beasts had come to them bearing gifts and were subdued with hardly any resistance. The first batch was cull mostly—women, children and elders—useless for the fields. The men were apparently off on a hunting expedition. Revealing a surprising cunning I had not anticipated from them, my barbarians set a trap to capture the more valuable natives. Just as a good fisherman exploits a minuscule catch to lure larger fish, my barbarians corralled their captives in a clearing, bound them tightly together and, with their trap baited, they hid.

The hunters soon returned, mounting a formidable rescue attempt. A violent volley of musket fire and the threat of another, aimed at their captured kin, forced them to succumb. Makeshift ropes held the slaves at the moment. The messengers had been dispatched to fetch the irons—and their captain.

I was overwhelmed. Truly, I thought, God intended my success. He had delivered me safely to this bounteous place and presented my first shipment as an offering. Such was my evil conceit, I confess that I nearly dropped to my knees in prayer for the gratitude I felt. The men gathered the irons. I accompanied them to the site. It was a brief journey, just into the river and around the first bend. And there they were, tied together at the neck, wrists behind their backs, awaiting the inspection of the False Priest.

Eager to assess my prize, I jumped the bow, before the boat scraped sand, wading ashore. The natives sensed I was the leader as I emerged from the water. I felt their primitive, searing gazes. Hatred boiled in them all. It was disconcerting. I had never seen slaves before they had been broken of their fight and silently wondered whether they would ever be shaken of this palpable rage. A quick observance that their knots were taut, and a glance to the loaded muskets pointed at their heads, reassured me but little.

Despite their venomous stares, I was impressed with the captives. I estimated by quick count, over two hundred in all. Tall sinewy physiques, with sun-browned hides and raven hair, was the rule for either gender. The men were more muscular of course, but any of the women would have sported a worthy fight had we allowed them opportunity. Were it not for the clothing—such as it was—and their hair style, I would honestly have found difficulty distinguishing them. They dressed similarly and sparsely, nearly as naked as their animal kin, a testimonial to their lowly nature. Downing naught else but the sheerest loins, the women supplemented their modesty only slightly with a sash over their bosom tied with cord at the neck and back. In all, their tan flesh was their principle wardrobe.

The men wore their hair in a knot, nearly atop their heads; the women employed no constraints, combing the dark locks straight well below the shoulders.

Oh, but their powerful builds were a marvel!

All natives we encountered thus far appeared of the same clan. Despite their resemblance, I was convinced my newly-acquired property was of a different tribe than the armada seen earlier at the large river. Perhaps, I reasoned, they comprised a faction that had broken away. I reached this judgment because the men bore none of the body paintings of their kin to the north. Interestingly, they boasted no adornment at all. The only décor of note was a marking of what appeared to be a fish with its mouth agape on the thigh of some women.

I attributed the design to be of no importance, classifying it as the residue, no doubt, of some pagan ritual. The markings did attract my attention sufficiently to admire the well-formed figures of the female slaves. They were truly beautiful. Strong, exotic, emanating an animalistic allure that surpassed merely their scanty garb; my blood boiled at the sight of them. I am not, after all, truly a priest and I had been a sea quite a long time.

Upon reflection, which is all that is left me on this accursed vessel, a doubt—not conscience, for I had none—but a nagging voice of *warning* that I should have heeded, imposed itself on me, dictating a show of caution. This instinct had

faithfully served me in the past and I would have done well to
follow its counsel. But as I said, the natives were beautiful so,
to my doom, I ignored it.

Decreeing captain's pleasure, I singled out one particularly voluptuous captive and demanded that she be delivered
to my quarters. My ruffians scowled at this. They had strict
orders to minimize their contact with any captives, lest they
damage my property, but I felt no such constraint.

"Was this not *my* property?" I reasoned.

The native girl struggled fiercely, as would any other
trapped frightened animal, ferociously resisting their advances.
Fearing that the temperaments of my barbarians would ruin
the attractive features of my selected prize, I approached the
girl … A child really, tho' woman she was, in age and beauty,
her savage mind could never achieve the sophistication of the
true gentler sex.

She was a parody to me, a resource, a lie. She was a posses-
sion I now owned and could employ in any manner I saw fit.
No harm that befell her would have troubled me any more
than if a horse were whipped, or a sheep slaughtered for the
evening's meal. But my intended uses required her beauty.
Making a show of indignation, I shouted the two buffoons
mishandling the girl to halt, chastising them loudly for their
ineptitude. The brutes were confused, unable to grasp the blunder they had committed, for indeed they had none to grasp.
Nonetheless, fearing my blade, they accepted the barrage docilely.

This infuriated me to no end. Their cowed demeanor
threatened to blunt my attempted ruse with the girl. To salvage my prize I had to act quickly. Drawing my cutlass out of
the hilt in one fluid motion, I caught the blade using the folds
of my robe and swung it, axe-like, bludgeoning each fool once
above the ear. I drew enough blood for effect, but I used the
handle, not the edge; their heads were hard, and my aim is
renowned.

I continued my performance, exploiting this scene to garner her trust, and when I turned to look at her I saw that I had attained it. I gently lifted her from the floor and undid her neck binding, but not her wrists. Monster that I am, I even mustered a reassuring smile that she meekly returned. Feigning anger, I delivered her to the brutes. In a ponderous voice I spoke words that held meaning different than their impressions, communicating to both the brutes and the girl;

"She will go with you quietly now. I have won her confidence. She has seen my display of bravado and thinks I am going to kill you if you harm her ... Be warned *señores* ... She is right. Take her to my quarters!"

As they nudged her away, I spied the fish marking on her thigh as well, but again, gave it no import.

I turned instead to the remaining crew. That the brutes had harvested a bounty was unquestioned, but one cannot clench the grip of discipline with kind words. I noted the arm of a native body jutting from a bush off to one side. Tracing it back, I found the casualties of the natives' assault piled in a heap; twenty men of a productive field age in all, fatal musket wounds tagging the lot of them. The ships' hold could accommodate one hundred more if the slaves were packed effectively.

"These dead men would have served me better in irons. As corpses they are worthles," I scolded my crew, disdainfully. One surly sailor, the bravado of having survived battle clouding his better judgment, voiced his displeasure at my harsh words, as I hoped one would.

"They attacked us viciously. We had no recourse. Of course if, perhaps, the great False Priest fought with us, we might have fared better—"

Without hesitation, in mid-phrase, the stupid cocky expression still locked on his face, I ran him through with my cutlass. My aim is always true. I skewered him cleanly through the heart and he was expired before I had removed my weapon.

As the dead man slumped, I snatched off the cross he wore around his neck, draped his body on my shoulders and tossed him on the pile of slaughtered natives.

"I have no use for a dead slave or a rebellious crewman. And the False Priest does not keep what he does not need …"

Turning to head back to the ship, I hoisted the cross on my bloodied cutlass and added, "And may the devil protect the man who tries to bury that pig because, as you can see, God certainly cannot."

Dumbfounded, my barbarians remained in locked immobility, hopelessly tangled in the latticework of terror and profound hatred I wove. If any could have killed me then, they would have done so eagerly. As it stood, they meekly grumbled and dispersed, retreating from my reach under one weak guise or another. I paid them no heed and, in fact, turned my back to them in contempt, comfortable that none among them was so foolhardy as to exploit my inattention. I think I even chuckled aloud as I made my way back to the boat.

My chosen female companion was propped up at the bow, a glorious figurehead adorning my modest vessel. She was scanning the horizon, with her back to me. The soft afternoon land breeze had blown the thick, straight, raven hair off her bronze skin and I admired the smooth, toned frame which, but for the sliver of cord fastening her garments, was completely exposed for all eyes under the blazing sun to see.

I longed to sit beside her but her two brute escorts, oars at the ready, formed a wall between us. I could not scale the filthy, broad-shouldered barrier without considerable clumsy maneuvering in the tiny boat and did not wish to lose my aura of dignity in that attempt. Selecting instead the stern plank, I gruffly ordered the brutes to push off. My seating, rather than beside a gloriously beautiful woman, put me in a direct line with the grunting faces of the rowing brutes. To classify my mood as disappointed would be a grotesque understatement, but the journey to the ship was a short one and, despite the haste evident in this document which suggests the contrary, I am a patient man.

As we maneuvered the river to the mouth, I squeezed occasional peeks at my prize between dirty shoulders. Though she must have been quite uncomfortable, she had not moved from her stance, back still to me, intensely searching the waters. What must have she been thinking as my mighty vessel emerged as her destination? Truly, I thought, this beautiful savage would be awed into a compliant mood. I would be a god to her, or so I led myself to believe. I even held the preposterous notion that she had her back to me because she dreaded my gaze. I sadly know, too well now, that I was no god. She communed with *true* heavenly beings and her attention was toward their eyes, not away from mine.

As we approached the ship, I witnessed what I thought was a vision. I swore that I saw a native floating in the water. He looked directly at my prize and gestured with his hands. My prize seemed to nod her head in the slightest of acknowledgments and he disappeared under the surface, leaving not a ripple. He never resurfaced. My brutes had their backs to the event and the girl was unreliable, so I reasoned that the water's shimmer played a trick on me, or that I must have dozed.

How pathetic am I that such a brazen warning was discarded. Oh, the bounty of signs that I missed completely. The clues that I gave no merit. The stupidity of my arrogance! Had I but considered broadening my perspective beyond my narrow, closed circle, I may have been spared this woe. In my defense, how was I, a *pirate*—naught but a parasite of the open waters—to fathom the wonders that God was capable of?

But I have strayed in my prose to self pity.

The boat was moored and we boarded. Not trusting the free hands of a savage, the girl was lifted to the deck.

"Take her to my quarters and offer her the fine blue dress from the large chest with the ruby handles. There is a small painting of a woman wearing a similar garment on my wall. Show it to her until you are certain she understands my expectation. Undo her bindings and leave her to prepare, but make certain that my door is locked … I will gut the buffoon so abysmally inept that he allows a savage to slip from his grasp."

The brutes immediately set out to follow my orders. The first extended his arm to shove my prize roughly in the direction he wanted her to move but his partner, a slightly less dim brute, was quicker. Remembering my response to their mishandling, he deflected the blow and, with the saddest of forced smiles, gently turned my prize and nudged her softly towards my cabin. In a short moment, the first brute understood and he, too, cracked the stupid smile. He even tried patting the girl on her head in the manner of a beloved pet. They moved her off and, with the skeleton crew I left on board preparing the hold below decks for its living cargo, I was left to my own company. I took stock of my progress.

My plan was assembling itself seamlessly. I had conquered many of the foreseen obstacles with little resistance and there was naught else I imagined would harbor more peril than the odd skirmish. My claimed property had fought, true to their savage namesake. I resigned that my outpost would lose many brutes in achieving their quotas, but brutes were easily replenished. Ale and lies had filled this expedition and both still ran freely in the harbor towns of Europe.

Then there was the omnipresent risk of a return across the Atlantic expanse, which only fools ventured lightly. Still, the Atlantic had always faithfully delivered me and I had no cause to think she would be of a mood to turn her favor away. Overrunning as I was with this unprecedented success, I actually strutted the decks.

Had anyone seen me, I would have been quite a sight. Prancing to and fro', my ugly, deep brown, sweat-caked robes swishing about as I spun. Whipping my blade through the air, I danced the decks, a carefree expansive, ballet. But as I mentioned, there were no witnesses to my arrogance and, lacking an audience to boast for, it did not last. Breathless and giddy, chuckling between gasps, my jig ended at the port side where the shore of the vast unknown continent, silhouetted by the orange sunset sky, halted me, sucking away my cheer.

"So pristine." I thought.

"So unknown."

"So much I am ignorant of in there."

I confess to succumbing at that moment to an uneasy sensation. I worried. Preparation and audacity were the armaments of my success. One required knowledge to properly prepare and I had so little. Compensating for my deficits with outrageous bravado had convinced a Duke and some brutes, but *I* was not so fortunate as to succumb to my own ruse. Had I anticipated enough? I know for certain now, in obvious ruin, that I had not, but discussing my concerns would reveal them. Concerns lead to doubts and a rogue brazen leader does not show doubt. That night, as with all nights previous, I was my only counsel ... I and the sea creatures congregating beneath my ship.

All around, darting in and out of sight, long thin streaks striped the waters; the unmistakable signs of dolphins below the surface. I marveled at their numbers and chuckled, wondering what advice they would lend?

Ironic, is it not, that I know that answer?

I could not help but observe that their paths, while wide and erratic, favored my ship; revolving in spiraling loops around my keel, occasionally even bumping with sufficient force for the vibrations to pass through the decks to my sandals. I reasoned that I had anchored over a favorite feeding place and they were expressing their displeasure. Here was yet another new phenomenon: bold, aggressive dolphins. I shuddered to contemplate that the land I brashly invaded was so exotic that even the playful companions of the open seas were different.

They were dangerous. What other dangers I wondered? What other dangers indeed.

Dismissing my melancholy with more feigned bravado, a commodity I never found lacking, I prescribed myself an evening of rum and a beautiful savage as a remedy for my trepidation, and stormed boldly to my quarters.

As I expected, my buffoons were actively guarding my prize … in a manner. Backsides completely unguarded, they were crowding the crack on my thick oak door trying to peak through. The idiots' rumps presented an opportunity too tempting to avoid. With my blade already firmly in hand, I delivered one sharp smack broadside (which in truth sounded much worse than the actual damage), scattering them to their posts. Not daring to rub their wounds, they stood teetering at tense, clumsy, dumbfounded attention. Given the treasure waiting within my chambers, I had no stomach to bear their presence so close.

"Get out of my sight." I whispered as I relieved them of my key and unlocked the door. Sore as they were, tired too, I swear so rapid was their departure that they were vanished before the lock clicked open. Preparing for the sight awaiting me, and the dangers she presented, I held my sword hand at the ready as I pulled open my door.

She wore the dress. That was my first impression. But I belittle the vision by speaking so plainly of her radiance. She wore the dress the way it was supposed to have been worn and the way it would never be worn again. Standing at the balcony, framed by the crimson sunset sky, her tall, smooth, sinewy figure cut a fine outline. She was not cast in the soft, pasty mold my usual flavor of woman, the ladies-of-the-court, championed.

No spectator in the arena of the living was she. Forged she was in the robust, healthy, smithy fires of a participant. Raven black hair, plumb straight, cascading over her broad, attractive, bronze bare shoulders and down along the fringes of the blue fabric she so magnificently adorned. Her eyes trembled but, to my delight and slight discomfort, they did not avert their gaze.

She was not *beautiful*—she was beauty. Paralyzed, I gasped. I was ... stunned!

Then the bravado took command. I entered my cabin, locking the door behind me, and she backed a step closer to the banister. I considered chasing her down but, as I mentioned, she was quite healthy and I may have harmed her beauty, or worse—torn the dress—if forced to subdue her. I was certain she feared me enough to attempt the insane. To salvage my evening's entertainment, I chose to seduce rather than conquer. Forcing myself to ignore her, I retrieved a half-bottle of fine rum from underneath a loose stack of charts and a pair of dusty glasses from an old chest which belonged to the original owner of this vessel before his untimely demise (at my hand of course) willed it to me. With careful calculation, I poured two glasses and, extending one, I ever so slowly decreased the gap between us.

Oh, the delight I felt when she did not move away. I smiled and cooed with my most sincere voice, telling her how beautiful she was. I spoke of the many vile and terrible acts I would commit on her and her fellow beasts but I did so with a tone intended to lull her into — if not trust, exactly — a sense of guarded interest. In this manner, I reached to just beyond arms' length, cup still extended.

Gingerly, having never seen glass before I gather, my savage beauty accepted the drink. She touched the lip and handle with her fingers, poking at various sections. Sniffing the contents, her face contorted peculiarly, not in revulsion so much as curiosity. Recognizing that alcohol was a strategy for dismantling her resistance, I held my cup as example, took the softest of sips, and motioned for her to do the same.

She did not respond. I continued demonstrating with less and less patience until my cup was dry and still the stupid creature did not understand. I decided to give her one other glass; then I would simply attack, risks to the dress and her beauty be damned. I remember how her eyes brightened when I poured the rum from the bottle.

She was fascinated by the bottle, even taking a measured step towards me to inspect it closer. I was confused at her interest, but it was progress, so I held it out for her. She attempted to hold it, but I would not let it go. This was not the barreled ferment I dispensed to the crew, but my refined personal stock, collected in a sculpted stoneware container. She had not touched her rum, and with the long journey ahead I had no desire to see her spill my stores. She did not like this, and retracted her advance.

Then she did the most curious thing. Mirroring me perfectly (to the habit I seem to have of extending my little finger as I drank), she downed her cup's contents in one swig and extended her empty cup towards the bottle.

I was delighted. Her message was crystalline and I was only too happy to oblige. I stepped up to her, pressing close. She did not move back. I remember, she even favored me with the most devastating of smiles, a delicious trusting grin, which enhanced her already striking features. Had I not seen for myself, I would have sworn it impossibe for her to be more beautiful. Yet she was.

She still held out the cup. I held out my bottle to pour for her and I was undone.

Her speed was spectacular. In one movement, she released her cup, counting on its fall to attract my attention. Then, grasping the neck of the bottle, she spun quickly, wrenching it from my grip. I swear to you now that I felt no pain, merely a dull whump on the side of my head. My cabin seemed to lurch right and I compensated by leaning left. And again, by all I that know now is truly holy, I did not feel pain.

But I was horizontal, on my side and immobile, staring paralyzed at the open balcony. Conscious, capable of the slightest of head movements but little else, I was reduced to a helpless witness, watching the drama unfold in my own quarters. My attacker violently tore her dress off, tatters of the delicate fabric floated hypnotically in the still air. She had retained her native clothes (such as they were) as undergarments, needing only a minor reattachment of the cords.

Restored to her feral attire, she invested one last satisfied verification of my incapacitation, and leapt boldly onto the banister. The wind caught her hair as she crouched forward, leg muscles tightening, preparing for her jump overboard ...

But, she did not move.

Clearly this hesitation was not her desire. Even I, in clouded stupor and the source of her revulsion, was keenly aware that every fiber of her being ached to be free of my ship. She had been instructed to remain by someone outside. I wondered who commanded the girl and precisely where they were. Nothing but water deep enough for my laden keel to clear surrounded us and, dumb as my brutes were, even they would have thwarted an intruder approaching the ship.

An argument ensued. I did not understand it. The girl's language, an archaic blend of vowels, whistles and growls translated to nonsense in my ears, and was whispered anyway. That she wished to abandon my ship was evident from her frantic gesturing. I heard nothing from the conversant in the waters to whom she pled her argument passionately, but as her shoulders slumped, it was apparent she had lost.

As if in consolation, a spear—smooth gray shaft, sporting a glimmering pink and white tip—flew up to her and she caught it expertly with both hands. Dropping from the banister, landing animal-like on both feet, yet enticing not a sound from the rickety decks, she wielded the spear in an attack stance that was quite familiar to her. Too late for any action but utter amazed acknowledgment, I then understood my vanity had not plucked a frightened maiden, but a warrior. One who had just received orders from her mysterious superiors, and was as adept in carrying them out as I was helpless to prevent her.

She moved beyond my ability to follow with my eyes. Then I blacked out or she struck me anew because in my next recollection, I was bound hand and foot—with my robe nowhere in sight. Twisting to seek the whereabouts of the devil who imprisoned me in my own cabin, I saw through the rising sun leaking in that I was alone.

I heard much commotion on the deck. My crew had come aboard. Their rowdy, excited chatter drowned my screams for attention until one of them dared to knock on my cabin.

The fool actually inquired if "Everything was all right?"

Compromised as I was, I suppressed my rage at their utter stupidity sufficiently, to inform them that "Everything was NOT all right," and to command that they break through. Using the stone-solid mahogany table in the galley, they splintered my door, freeing me from the ridiculous position I endured.

A brute held out my mangy disguise, even managing a smile. I would have gutted him, so angry was I, but for the absence of my cutlass.

Between grunts and apologies, I gathered that the girl had escaped my clutches and, with my own robe as a disguise, had freed the five slaves originally deposited in the hold. Somehow, without a boat, she and the five had managed to reach shore where in stealth, they in turn freed my remaining property. Taken by surprise, and outnumbered by a factor of five, my brutes were overrun and retreated to the ship. All was lost.

One lone, feral female demon had unraveled my success in its entirety. My rage was blinding. No calculation, no strategy, no plan came to mind other than finding that little cur and seeing that she rued the day she danced with the False Priest.

I boiled over.

"To arms you scurvy rats!" I bellowed, breaking out the muskets.

"Raise anchor, move this ship to the river mouth. Let them taste our cannons!"

To the others I ordered, "Man the boats; Two muskets each. Pack as much dry powder as you can carry. Prepare to slaughter any animal that survives our volley. We will wipe clean the stain of this insult with the blood of their entire herd!"

My crew shuddered. They had no desire to reengage their attackers. I had not been present to witness the ferocity of either encounter, but my headcount acknowledged it was severe. A third of my crew was missing, I presumed fatally. What remained was bloodied and afraid to a man. Only a stronger fear of my wrath would entice them to return.

So be it.

A shoulder to my nearest crewman's chest shot him overboard. His childish scream snuffed instantly as he plunged below the water. Grasping the next man by his collar, I flung him over as well, but not before relieving him of his cutlass, with which I turned to the rest.

To the others, my anger seething between clenched teeth, I methodically repeated my orders, crisply pronouncing each word in a tone whose finality was accented by the sloshing and pleading emanating from the water.

"Raise … anchor … move … this … ship … to … the … river … mouth … Man … the … boats … two … muskets … each … NOW! YOU MANGY WORTHLESS SACKS OF RANCID MEAT!"

Of the two desperately swimming men, I added, "Fetch muskets for them. If they live, you may retrieve them on your way to the shore … Carry out my orders or by all that is unholy, I will run the lot of you through!"

And so we moved in with my aggressive dolphins in tow. I was beyond reasoning. I was beyond thought. I was in a pit of my own design and construction — a vile chasm lined with my sins of arrogance, cruelty, hatred, and greed.

I took the helm shrieking out orders to scurrying brutes tripping over themselves to comply or face my retribution.

Truly, I know not which felt more unfortunate—those who manned the boats in anticipation of yet another losing battle with the natives, or the hapless crew who remained onboard within my grasp.

My ship lurched forward, creaking uncomfortably as it ploughed the shallower regions. The dolphins' pounding increased in both frequency and amplitude. I ventured further than a saner man would have dared and, upon laying sight of their accursed village, turned hard about to expose the shore to my broadside. Barking more than speaking, I redirected my crew to the port cannons. As they loaded, I leapt on the upper gunwale in mockery of the female cur who bludgeoned me, and spewed the vilest profanities I could conjure. I cursed the natives. I cursed the girl, the land, their idiotic dolphins, the duke who had sent me on this fool's errand, and noting the annoying absence of cannon fire, the wretches who tried my patience.

I was more than mad. I was a raving lunatic.

The thunder of cannons did not assuage this lunacy. It merely transferred it to a maniacal glee. I giggled like a happy child as tree and structure exploded to dust in front of me.

"RELOAD!" I laughed. "Empty the magazines on them. They will know this day the meaning of crossing the False Priest! But they will know it for only a short while!"

Shot after deafening shot shattered the morning air. The bombardment upturned every aspect of the natives' existence. The cannons overlooked little. Their village and the forest surrounding it flattened under the barrage. Splintered trees cracking louder than the weapons which annihilated them, crashing recklessly into other trees, then onto huts. Fires broke out, adding to the chaos.

The devastation was complete. No creature could have survived such a bombardment. And still, foolishly I shrieked the cannons onward. With no thought to the consequences, I waged my war on the accursed continent itself, disarming my ship with every firing, relenting only when the powder kegs were drained. Spent and restless, I fell as silent as the cannons.

The shore was masked in a blanket of smoke that lazily drifted our way with the land breeze. Damaged permanently was I, from exposure to that earsplitting cannon fire. A persistent phantom ringing, that remains with me still, underscored the crackles of the flame licks, the grunted breathing of my brutes, and the accursed banging of the wretched dolphins accompanying the enveloping approach of the smoke. Pungent smells of burning foliage and powder stung my nostrils.

All but the smoke was still as death when, leaping out of the very water, her spear arm tightly coiled, a lone native girl attacked my ship. She had launched from below around where the dolphins congregated, rising many feet above the surface, dragging a curtain of water in her wake. Her appearance was similar to my cur. In truth, the long, straight black hair, and pleasant sinewy features at first gave me the impression it was she, but this one was fairer of skin tone, and she wore garments of a silken gray rather than the tanned hides I had noted. We all watched her seemingly float in the air, mesmerized and unable to move.

As the water she dragged up with her draped away, the splendor of her magnificent form was revealed. Then it was certain she was not of the land tribe at all. By all that I now know is holy, I gazed upon the physique of a half woman, half fish. But not a fish, for her tail moved back and forth ... like a whale's ... or a dolphin's.

Too late did I realize the secret of the aggressive dolphins. Before the waters pulled her back, the creature unleashed her spear, impaling a wretch and stirring a panic in my ranks. They did not have time to regain composure because, immediately following the marvel we witnessed, ten more blasted upwards, spears at the ready, and ten more wretches fell.

Panicked retreat from the ship's gunwale saved the remainder from the next volley. Perched at the upper deck, away from the cannons, I was at the moment above their attention, and bore paralyzed witness to the choreographed elegance of the water creatures' onslaught. Hundreds of moving bodies were circling below. Regularly, ten would break off from their congested swarm. They would align themselves with a portion of my ship and, with a wondrous velocity, they would launch themselves in unison many feet out of the waters, discharge their spears, and descend to the swarm again. While they all broke the surface in synchronization, their final altitudes varied, perhaps by their individual ability, or from some predetermined agreement on their target, I could not say.

Of their appearance, I can relate quite detailed descriptions. Frozen from incredulity, I did naught else but stare in awe at them.

Male and female equally proficient with their weapons they were. Of the weapon itself, a spear of fine craftsmanship, wielded with deadly accuracy. The rattle of their impact on the wooden deck hinted they were of a light stone. An errant throw landed near my position, and I inspected it. Lighter than I anticipated from its strength, the head, pink, and razor sharp, fixed to the shaft with a powerfully strong adhesive I could not discern, nor detach. Their upper torsos were quite similar in size and shape to the shore natives, truly, as if they were kin; and like their land brethren, they too wore very little. Some had pouches they strapped to their shoulders, I spied a decorative necklace or two; the women concealed their modesty with splotched gray or black garments that I gathered were made from some felled aquatic creature's pelt.

Two grotesque gashes adorned either side of the creatures. Deep and wide they were, gushing water, cleaved from spine to chest, daylight visible through portions of the body, where none should have been present. They pulsated rapidly, four horrible mouths vomiting water.

I had at first, mistakenly, thought my wretches actually inflicted them as counterblows, but all the creatures exhibited them with no apparent discomfort, and my wretches had not displayed any fight worth mentioning. Their tails were long and inordinately flexible, sometimes bending to touch the head as they arched to prepare their return to the waters. The flukes, ridged with a knobby core, displayed an amazing versatility. Functioning as would a fine Spanish courtier's fan, they opened and closed to suit the needs of their propulsion magnificently. As they pumped their tails for speed, I spied a wide paddle form under the waves which instantly compressed into a narrow tip right before their launch.

My initial impression that they were fair of tone was only partially accurate. While their face and frontage did seem pale in relation to what I had come to expect from a native, their backsides were sun-baked brown.

They were beautiful.

And they were destroying us. A sloppy retreat below, away from the spear gauntlet emptied the decks of all but the mortally wounded and myself. Lacking anyone to aim for, the attacks ceased. I wondered why I had not been fired upon. Granted my perch on the upper deck gunwale elevated me by several feet, but many leaps I had observed could easily have scaled to my height. Had they not seen me? Did my separation from the cannons dismiss my danger to them? Was I not worth a spear?

Screams and musket fire from the boat crews snapped my attention astern. I had forgotten the wretches in the small boats. The creatures had capsized one of them and were methodically dispatching its inhabitants who could do naught else but tread water and pray for mercy. One by one they disappeared, pulled below in an instant, never to surface again.

The others, quick to realize their eminent danger in the small vessels, had managed to crawl back onboard my ship. They joined the injured who escaped the spear gauntlet huddled below decks. Realizing my only chance of surviving the fate enveloping me lay with them, I worked my way cautiously down to their position.

Cutlass in hand, the very waters around me now my enemy, I listened hard for sounds that would announce an attack. None was uttered. I made the move unmolested. Inside, gazing at the dead eyes of my wretches, I despaired. All was lost. There was no fight left in them. A few still clutched their undischarged muskets uselessly in their trembling hands. Cutlasses dangled unattended in their sheaths. They were sheep awaiting the bludgeon of the butcher.

I had, throughout our entire voyage, driven them to the brink of their limited sanity. There, at the precipice of human tolerance, held in place by the aura of fear I projected, they had toiled. The water creatures had shoved them over the edge.

The pounding from below continued.

How long we stared at one another with the rhythmic whumps resonating between us, I do not recollect. A loud, ugly, slow creak finally broke the paralysis and we lurched suddenly to starboard, sliding the lot of us mercilessly against the wall. We began taking in water. I mustered one last burst of bravado.

"On your feet you mangy sheep! You three, get below, seal the hull with whatever you can find. Use barrels, chests, your dead crewmates if you have to, but get this ship watertight! We are sitting high. The creatures must have dumped some ballast. We can use that to our advantage. Slide and secure our stores on the port side. We can skim over the shallows without risking the keel. The rest of you, on deck, anchors up, set full sails, trims be damned. We will depart this purgatory and live to tell about it!"

And to myself only, I added "And never return to this abomination of a continent."

Any fate was more tolerable if a man felt he was fighting. They leapt into action. I took the helm and soon a lunge set us on our course. When the ship began moving, the creatures' attacks ceased. Their absence was welcomed, but sat uneasy, for if we did not know where they were; they could be anywhere.

We limped battered but unmolested back to the open sea. I was down to such a skeleton of a crew; I dared not even risk pulling the life boats up. They trudged along, moored to my ship, bumping and skidding over one another. Eventually, to my joy and relief, we circled the barrier island and were in the open waters.

We had food, water, and sufficient crew to make for Spain. Lacking powder to defend ourselves and ballast for stability in high winds, we were however at the mercy of god, devil, water creature, warships and my comrade pirates. Our prospects were not keen, but at the moment, we were content merely to have them.

I had incinerated my ambitions to live out my days as a gentleman with my insane attack on the natives' village.

But, we lived.

I lived.

Had I not risen to my reputation from much lower beginnings than where I now rested? Returning to Spain was inconceivable. The ire of the disappointed duke would have been too formidable a force to avoid. England, however, was a rising power, and quite ambitious in its desire to dominate the seas. Perhaps I would offer my services to her crown. But not in exchange for land and title; instead I would ravage the Spanish and Portuguese shipping lanes in the role I performed best.

Was I not the False Priest? Did I not just survive the attack of water demons and live to tell the tale? For a hefty fee, I would gladly fly the British colors below my own, carrying out all their orders save one.

I would not ever again return to this accursed continent.

Basking with the survivor's delight, I steered my ship to the great current which would take us to the British Isles and daydreamed of becoming an English ally. Exhausted I must have been, because I failed to notice the wretches surrounding me until a swift movement deprived me of my sword.

They must have attacked in unison. I was smothered beneath a stinking writhing pile of humanity and could scarcely breathe. I heard them shout:

"Get his hands!"

"Tie his hands!"

"And his feet and arms as well. He's a slippery one he is. Be generous with the rope."

"Aye, but save some for his neck!"

In moments I was a bruised bundle of knots and flax. Pushed beyond tolerance, the wretches had finally mustered sufficient courage to mutiny. I took little solace in the fact that it required their entire number to overpower me.

A debate on what to do with me ensued. Their propositions ranged from the brutish to the creative, but the common thread was that all were quite painful and irreversibly fatal. The core arguments revolved around which of their suggestions would produce the most discomfort. I allowed this to proceed until I detected a waning of their fury, then I reestablished who I was.

"Cowards!" I yelled. "Cowards, the lot of you! Argue until your very faces are blue. You will not carry out any of these ridiculous fantasies. Not a one of you has the stomach for it. Now enough of this pathetic bravado. Only I have the knowledge to steer us back to Europe. Only I know the use of the compass and how the stars point. Only I know the currents and breezes.

"Without me, you will be lost in the waters, or worse, you will steer directly into the path of the Spanish Armada who are quite eager to get their clutches on the crew of this ship. Release me now and, because we have survived an ordeal of unusual circumstances, I will overlook this. Release me later, as you know you must, and I will not be so merciful."

I stared them down, studying the faces of my mutineers for weakness, confident that, as in the previous challenges, I would find it and persevere. The tension lingered and then the unexpected occurred. They burst into laughter. Roaring, unfettered, loud and raucous, they carried on. The horrors each had endured dissolved with the mirth, transforming my battle-worn wretches to a bunch of mates at an inn having heard the funniest joke in their entire lives. And, upon reflection, they truly had. Bound, disarmed, outnumbered, my intimidation was as empty as the hold below. How could I have been a threat?

My masquerade disintegrated. The False Priest was dead. I was once more only Francisco Emilio Sabatez DeCarta, a helpless, pathetic charlatan.

In time, the laughter died down and, without comment to me, for I was no longer of any import, they ransacked the captain's cabin and found the gold I had so greedily hoarded through the years. The laughter returned to its previous crescendo, for they realized that with their diminished numbers, splitting my booty would provide a comfortable life for them all. Assuming they survived the sea voyage, they could live the remainder of their days in splendid anonymity.

A bottle of my good rum emerged, ironically the very same which the cur bludgeoned me with, and they all shared a drink, toasting their new fortune. They produced my well-annotated charts and, to my amazement, a few of them could actually translate my writings.

Working together, they set their course. From what I overheard, it was not a bad deduction. Their chances of reaching Europe were fair.

Nightfall came and they threw me onto this dismal craft. It was the only one of the six boats afloat after the pounding escape. They stocked it with the one item from my quarters that they found of no value—the chest where this stationary was stowed. And while they did supply a skin of water, they did not even provide me with an oar, nor did they afford me the courtesy of untying my bindings.

Instead they tossed part of the blade of my cutlass. As a final indignity, they smashed it to pieces. I watched my ship, my fortune and my chances for survival shrink and disappear over the horizon without emotion. I was beaten; resigned to accept the pirate's fate, dying alone and poor, betrayed by my own crew the instant I was not strong enough to stop them. I fell into a deep, fitful slumber which lasted until the sun was high the next day.

Had I perished that evening, my soul would have plummeted to the fires where I would make eternal payment on my sins. I wish to my very marrow that I had. For when I awoke, my bindings had mysteriously been cut away. I was still in a woeful predicament, but the freedom of movement stoked an ember of hope. The seas were calm. The currents were familiar. My craft, a beaten sorry, but still seaworthy thing, creaked gently with the bobbing waves. I ventured a sip of the water—stale, but potable for some days yet.

Though my stationary chest held nothing of note, I could stuff the sheets of my journals into any cracks that might arise. I was holding the chest thinking to somehow convert the iron and wood into an oar, when one of the creatures who defeated us so completely, lunged out of the water and into my craft.

I reacted instinctively, crashing the chest on the side of its head near the temple. The creature tried to block my blow with an arm, but it was off balance and only partially deflected it. The force of my strike repelled it back to the sea, where it splashed loudly, but remained floating face down. A crimson cloud of blood stained the waters around the still form.

I had killed it.

My blow had caused the creature to drop the object it had been carrying onto the boat's deck. A smooth, cylindrical, gray-green container the length of my forearm and of a diameter wider than my outstretched hand, lay on its side. A veined crack wrapped the circumference, liquid seeped from various points. I reached over to inspect my newly acquired inventory. As I raised it, the cracks succumbed and the container shattered. Cool, clean drinking water poured onto my hands and lap. It tasted sweet and fresh. The container had been full.

Had I but kept it whole, its contents might have extended my life long enough to reach the merchant lanes off Portugal. Like a dog, I dropped to the floor, trying to lap up the spilled contents, but it had already mingled with the caked salts and was useless. Just a few scant drops remained in the container's shards.

My newborn hope, delivered by the arms of a creature that should by all accounts yield me no sympathy, literally evaporated away. That it or another like it had untied me as I slept was apparent. Had I merely checked my murderous nature for just a moment, it would have handed me my salvation. Instead, the brute that I am, I slaughtered my savior.

Why did it do this?

I had invaded its waters, tormented its kin on the land, and would have committed unfathomable atrocities, had I not been bested in battle. My very crew had discarded me to the seas. I deserved and expected no mercy. Yet drifting slowly away from me was mercy embodied.

Why did I do this?

Though the sun was at full strength, and I had no shelter from its torment, a shiver ran through me. I felt shame. For the first time in my life, I had been shown kindness, and I had returned it with violence and suspicion. I realized then what these creatures were. The great artists of Florence were fools to have adorned God's angels with wings. Where in the sky could a holy host conceal itself? How could they influence their love from so lofty a perch? Angels did not don wings and halos, but tails and gills.

And they watched us, not from above on a cloud, but from the under the seas. Heaven was indeed all around us,

submerged below our grasp, but not beyond its reach. So elo-
quent was this revelation, so complete, that I broke to my knees
and prayed to God for forgiveness. Not the cathedral god with
tithes and titles, but the true God I now knew must exist. How
else could such benevolent magical beings come to be?

At first, I asked for nothing but the rapid ascension of the
beautiful, kind soul I had so callously extinguished. But as the
floodwaters of my regret gathered strength, I poured my life
into this lamentation. I asked for the forgiveness of all the
lives I had taken, for the repair of those souls I had tarnished,
and for the natives I so heinously attacked to rebuild their
peaceful existence. I know not how long my discord with God
lasted, but when it concluded, I was purged of my demons,
and my savior had disappeared. Perhaps an ocean predator
had snatched it away as a meal, or others of its kind had gathered it. I even harbored the thought I had perhaps not killed it
after all. Since I am destined never to know, I allowed myself
this one small hope.

Regardless, my angel was gone, as was my hatred.

It was then I took to penning this tale which you are now
concluding. I beseech you to heed my plea from the Neverworld
as you would if I were flesh and blood walking amongst you.
Do not trouble the natives of the large continent. They are
protected by angels who do not wish them disturbed. Do not
harm the angels. They are a gift God saw fit to deposit in the
seas. Who are we to question the Almighty? Do not live your
life in godless recluse. It is a hollow existence with an inevitable ending much like my own. Make peace with your life
before it is too late, and you may perhaps enjoy a frolic in the
seas with my angels when you reach the end of your journey
instead of burning next to me.

Heed my warning!

So says the ghost of Francisco Emilio Sabatez DeCarta—
He Who Was the False Priest

***

Addendum:

The attached document was found by fishermen in the hands of a dead man floating in a lifeboat off the coast of Portugal. Both the papers and the body were delivered to the Spanish Duke, Carlos the Black, in 1510. The Duke posted the dead man's head on a spike jutting from one of his towers. The journal was forwarded to the church where it was discredited on the premise that the writer was a heretic, and he expounded the idea of a heaven under the seas. Unusual for the day, this document was not burned for its heresy, but instead archived into anonymity.

Records of church personnel who have inspected this document before 1900 have long disappeared. It should be noted however that within three years of this document's delivery, Ponce De Leon "discovered" Florida, making landfall at roughly the same location as the document describes. De Leon, as fable would have it, sought the "Fountain of Youth," but that may have been a ruse for seeking another supernatural cache.

The Spanish interest in Florida, particularly with missionaries, was quite widespread and intensive, much more so than the clamor for territory acquisition warranted. A conclusion can be suggested that while Sabatez's claims were publicly scoffed, privately the church (or other parties with influence within the church) seriously considered them. Whether the church sought an alliance with the water creatures Sabatez alluded to or merely their destruction as abominations is a subject which should someday be addressed.

Many supporting documents verify the exploits of the False Priest and his disappearance from records coincides with this entry. There are also accounts of a scuttled Carrack similar in appearance to the chronicled descriptions of the False Priest's infamous vessel off the shore of England in 1509. Anecdotal accounts of a dozen Spanish gentlemen arriving at a township within a few days' walk of the wreck coincide with that date. Descendants of those Spaniards boast claims that the ancestors who settled there were escaped pirates.

The mention of Columbus falls in accordance with historic accounts.

Enrigo Vesperdi, Vatican Historian, 13 November 1921
Roberto DiBriccio, Translator, 9 March 1964

CHAPTER
8

Nathan's Problem

Saundra set the last pages of Sabatez's confession on the heaped coffee table stack. Then she quelled her "neat freak" demons by straightening and collating the document. She stretched a bit, rubbing her eyes. It felt late. Alone in the living room, muted voices and clinking dishes came from the kitchen.

"Three A.M.!" she moaned to herself, catching the wall clock's face.

"Why did Bernie do this to me? I have to be up in less than three hours!"

She rose stiffly and nearly fell over. Her right leg was asleep and would not respond to the weight. Catching herself on the armrest, Saundra hopped lightly until enough circulation returned to trust the leg's load-bearing capabilities again, and she hobbled to the kitchen.

They were all there—even Mom—engrossed in conversation and again ignoring her. But a bowl and a spoon were waiting and Bernie was opening the freezer to serve her.

"Dr. Sherban, I'm sorry, but I'm still not convinced. And I can't understand how you can be. How can you even trust a pirate?" Nathan asked.

"A dying pirate," Jane interjected.

"A dying pirate desperate to save his soul," Saundra added, leaping into the fray.

"A dying pirate desperate to save his soul *and delirious* from a few days in the sun without water," Nathan further stipulated.

Saundra loved it when Nathan argued. He was so passionate, and the acting and singing lessons so grounded, his comments seemed like mini-performances.

"Your point is legitimate Nathan. This guy was truly a bad man," Bernie replied.

"He dressed up like a priest to lure ships in and then he blew them out of the water! That's not 'bad.' Shoplifting is 'bad.' Speeding in a school zone is 'bad.' This guy was *evil*; with a life history of evilness. And I'm supposed to think he suddenly switches to remorse at the end? I don't think so."

Saundra felt she was missing something. She had obviously come in the midst of the discussion, but she failed to make the connection between Nathan's commentary and the story she just finished.

"How did you know that?" she asked Nathan.

"Know what? Oh, the blowing up other ships and stuff? Dr. Sherban gave us a quick bio on our False Priest while you finished up."

"Can I get a "Cliff's Notes" summary?" she asked, accepting the full bowl from Bernie.

"Sabatez started as an orphan," said Nathan. "His parents probably died in one war or another. This was around the time of the Spanish Inquisition. The Christians were trying to reclaim Europe by clearing out the last Moorish holdouts," he volunteered.

"He spent his childhood scrounging around seaport towns, living like an animal. Then as a young adult, he broke into a monastery. He was most likely looking for food, shelter, the poor box, whatever. He was definitely *not* looking for salvation ..."

"You don't *know* that," Bernie interrupted.

"But I don't *know* that," Nathan continued, corrected but adding under clenched teeth, "But I'm pretty convinced he wasn't."

And he barreled on before Bernie could interject again.

"Anyways. He stole a monk's robe, and put it on to keep warm. He walked around and noticed that the same townsfolk who used to treat him like an animal, kicking and throwing stuff at him, were all of a sudden really nice! And not just "we're not going to hit you anymore" nice, but genuinely nice. In the robe, he got a bunch of free meals, warm places to sleep, and he moved to the next town before they figured out his ruse. Sabatez did this for a while, until he got ambitious. He used his fake priest trick to get passage on a ship somewhere. After they were out to sea for a few days, he conned the crew into believing he was an emissary of the church sent to punish the heathens onboard and convinced the crew to mutiny. They commandeered the ship throwing all the passengers overboard. Sabatez declared himself captain and set out on a ten-year pirate adventure that ended up in the story you just put down. His fighting strategy at first was to plead for help using his disguise. Ships would see a crucifix hanging from his neck, and the robes, and they'd come close enough to be boarded with their defenses down. Enough folks survived to get the word out on the "poor little priest in peril" trick, so towards the end he became a more traditional pirate, but he never stopped wearing the robe. The guy even added a pair of crosses to the Jolly Roger … He was a monster. Is that about it Dr. Sherban?"

Bernie nodded in agreement.

"And you *know* this because … " Saundra queried.

"Because of another document I acquired," Bernie replied. "It provided the bio. Apparently in those days the Vatican had a crude version of the KGB. They kept tabs on everyone prominent enough to cause them worry … And Nathan, for the umpteenth time, please call me Bernie."

"Only if I can start calling Ms. Peterson 'Jane.'"

"No." responded Ms. Peterson.

"I got a bit of the suspicious stuff from the addendum. Sounds like they gave a lot of weight to the writing," Saundra said redirecting the subject.

"Yeah, but not how you think. That part was modern, inserted by the transcriber in '64," Bernie interjected. "Roberto DiBriccio was a really nice, older gentleman. He performed document translations back and forth in five languages for something like forty years, then he retired with his British wife. I got his name from a Cardinal who remembered reading some whacked-out memos involving mermaids back in the early seventies. The church had his number and he answered his phone on the first ring. I met him at his apartment in a Spanish "fishing-town-gone-tourist" called Fuengirola. He moved there as a compromise with his wife. She missed speaking English and he couldn't handle England's weather. The town's right on the Mediterranean's "*Costa Del Sol*,"[1] and there's a large expatriate British community. We had a great conversation over dinner and a phenomenal bottle of wine ... or two. He came across the Sabatez document as part of his workload. In translating it from Spanish to Italian and, later English, he became, and is still, utterly convinced the work was important and tried numerous times to get it moved up the chain for analysis but no one took him seriously.

We went back to his place and, over coffee, I read the copy of the transcript he'd "retained" illegally after he retired. That alone impressed me. Nobody steals from the church, especially not a pious career man like him. He must have really been convinced. DiBriccio also kept a notebook, filled an entire college ruled spiral binder with his meticulous crosschecks. He had done all the work the old-fashioned way too, slogging through hand-written card catalogs, obscure dusty books, and Microfiche strips. He really scoped the book out—tracking down every minute clue he could gather from the stationary maker, to the recorded weather at the alleged time, to the Duke's fate. Did I tell you all he was poisoned by his wife?"

Two nods and Saundra's shake later, Bernie continued, "Later on, just to be sure this soft-spoken, intelligent man wasn't a nutjob, I double-checked a lot of his data in a matter of a few hours by using Google. It's kind of amazing and sad, really, that forty years of slogging can be verified at one internet sitting. I found no inconsistencies worth noting ..."

"Besides the bit about the mermaids?" added Nathan sarcastically.

"Besides the bit about the mermaids, smart aleck. Oh, and just so you all know, I also tracked down the original Sabatez work and DiBriccio's official translation. I never asked to borrow the copy he made. I couldn't have used it anyway and I'd feel terrible if he got in trouble for illegally removing materials. You all just read the official church-certified version."

"The church knew about *homo aquaticus* five hundred years ago? So what are you suggesting? That they covered it up?" Saundra asked incredulously.

"Oh, come on," Nathan chimed in. "A church conspiracy? What—like the DaVinci Code?"

Saundra laughed. It was a funny notion. To her relief, Bernie smiled as well. "You're young Nathan. You haven't been exposed to enough bureaucracies to get a grasp of how truly inefficient they can become. Sabatez's work wasn't purposely suppressed. It was neglected. The Catholic Church runs an amazing empire, and they've been doing it for going on two thousand years. You have any idea how much stuff they have in their attics and closets? Vatican City was once only a church, then a complex, then a town … Now it's a sovereign nation. Can you imagine keeping track of all those things?"

"I don't even know where my keys are," Nathan admitted. The he quickly interjected, "But that's not the point!"

Throughout the discussion, Jane sat quietly. She rather enjoyed the conversation and felt no need to comment. Until now. "I've never seen you this argumentative Nathan. What is it about this that's bothering you so much?" she asked, curiously.

"That you can't *trust* the word of a monster! What's wrong with you? Can't you see that?" Nathan snapped.

He immediately caught himself, "I'm so sorry Ms. Peterson. I didn't mean to jump like that. I guess I'm just tired. I think yelling at my girlfriend's Mom is a clear signal that I need to call it a night." Nathan rose to leave, but Bernie stopped him.

"You can't leave like this. Tell me Nathan, do you acknowledge that the document was written by a dying pirate around five hundred years ago?"

Nathan nodded in agreement.

"And, given the discovery of Namor's skeleton, if this exact same document were written by a noble person—an *actual* priest, or a marooned merchant—for example, would you be this upset?" he asked.

"No, I guess not, but ..." said Nathan.

"Hang on ... And had Sabatez not been describing an attack by aquatic humans, and the subsequent murder of a merman, but the same events involving ordinary Native Americans escaping from a slave ship, would you have questioned it?" asked Bernie.

Nathan paused. He had to admit that he probably wouldn't have.

"So your only issue with Sabatez is the *homo aquaticus* ... Is that right?" pressed Bernie.

Nathan nodded.

"Keeping that in mind, then," said Bernie, smiling, "why don't you answer Jane's question *nicely* now. What *is* bothering you about this?"

Bernie proceeded to sum up the facts. "Every bit of evidence supports the writing. The wounds match. An iron and oak chest smashed on the side of the head would produce the temple injury, and the broken arm as well, if Namor tried to block the blow. The time-frame matches—right after Columbus, but before Ponce De Leon. The location matches. The Tomoka River is about five day's walk south of the Saint Johns. Even Sabatez's description of the heavily tattooed River Tribes matches.

"*This* is the guy who killed Namor. This is how he did it. This explains everything except how Namor wound up in that grave and where the land and water folks disappeared to. You're a bright guy Nathan. You know all this and you're still arguing ... So what *is* bothering you?" Bernie asked plainly.

Saundra watched the exchange mesmerized. She noted how masterfully Bernie helped guide Nathan's passionate ideas to a conclusion, and how he pulled back, returning to his ice cream, giving Nathan a space to assemble his reply. She hoped someday to have him teach her that gift. And with that thought in mind, she suddenly reached two important life decisions.

She would attend the University of Miami so she could study under him.

She, too, would be a PaleoBiologist.

Nathan responded finally, "It's just that if you're right and this holds true, a jerk who did nothing but garbage all his life is going to be *famous* just because he killed someone and then wrote down he was sorry. That is so *wrong* on so many levels!"

No one disagreed.

"It's like in performing," he continued. "I bust my tail every day (OK, I skipped today, but that was Dr. Sherban's fault). I pay my dues. I go to tryouts, auditions, and smoke the room. Everyone likes my work, and along comes this dufus who spent a week on a reality show, and bumps me for a role. Sabatez is like that dufus … I just don't like dufuses!"

Jane moved over to Nathan and kissed him on the cheek. "You're too idealistic Nathan. Don't ever change."

Nathan smiled, and returned the kiss with a light hug. He shook Bernie's hand, and Saundra walked him to the door, pausing only a moment to tap Sabatez's writing.

"Bernie, that was really cool of you to let us read this." he said.

"Good night Nathan," Bernie responded.

"'Night."

✳✳✳

Both teens missed a few periods of school the next day. Jane went to work, but kept nodding off at her desk. Bernie slept a few hours, but was hard at work on his laptop when Saundra awoke. She heard the softly clicking keys coming from the guest room.

She drove to school, arriving at the end of third period, staying after class to get missed work. Then she completed a lightning-shortened soccer practice where she and Jessica actually kidded around. Bernie was still clicking when she got home. She and Jane ate a quiet meatloaf and mashed potato dinner together and went to bed, leaving a plate in the microwave with a Post-It note:

> *"Nuke for about two minutes. Get some sleep!"*
> —*Saundra and Jane"*

The next day the note, the food, and Bernie were gone. Scrawled on a sheet of legal paper on the kitchen counter was a reciprocal note;

> *Hi,*
> *Meatloaf was great, had it cold as a sandwich. I slept*
> *four good hours. Sabatez was the last drop of written history.*
> *That well's dry. Got two meetings scheduled for Saturday and*
> *my gang's coming over to my place to clear out the paper*
> *clutter, so I can't come up Friday.*
> *I'm off to find UNwritten history*
> *See you next weekend.*
> *I'll call tonight.*
> *—Bernie.*

"What's UNwritten history?" Saundra asked aloud.

"That's a nerdy way of saying 'spoken,'" replied Jane. "Bernie's off to hear some stories."

CHAPTER
9

Road Trip

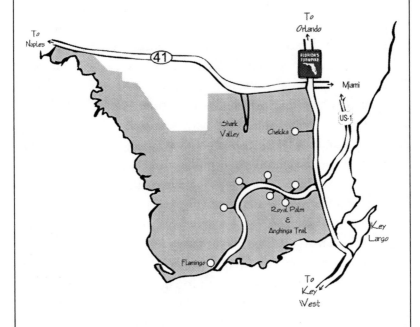

Everglades National Park: Florida
(author's favorite locations marked)

"Dr. Sherban, now that we're in the middle of a swamp, where anything you say won't affect your hippie-free-spirit-rebel-antiestablishment aura … I gotta say it … C'mon dude … a *minivan?*" Nathan joked

Saundra and Jane smiled. They had both been thinking the same thing since Bernie arrived in the uncharacteristically civilized silver grey vehicle to gather them that morning. Boarding the power EVERYTHING van, sinking into the plush adjustable captains chairs as the automatic doors whirred shut, enjoying surround sound Pink Floyd in their individually set temperature environments while the dual DVD players hummed into position, was the lap of luxury, especially when compared to the crank windowed, vinyl seating, AM station cabin of Bernie's decade old truck they had expected. Having made quite enough journeys in that rustic environment, Saundra and Jane boarded quietly, and without comment. Neither had any desire to jeopardize their reprieve and abandon their fortuitous bump to first class automotive comfort. It was however, an unusual mode for the unpretentious man they had grown to know so well.

"Would you all have preferred to make the two hour round trip in my truck?" Bernie answered a bit too defensively. "A colleague of mine needed to move some furniture. I needed to move some people. The trade was mutually beneficial. What seems to be the problem—other than sophomoric stereotypical demagoguery of a finely engineered vehicle? "

"Stereo … Demo … ?" muttered Nathan.

"He's saying that you shouldn't make fun of minivans just because they're minivans. Especially when enjoying their comforts," translated Jane.

"You really get nerdy when you're on the defensive," Nathan responded, a smile still creasing his face.

"You win. Next time the four of us go on a long trip, I'll get a 1965 Volkswagen love van with peace symbols and flowers all over it," Bernie answered.

"And wall to wall carpeting," Nathan added completing the gibe.

They drove on admiring the scenery in ergonomic air-conditioned splendor for a bit. Everglades colors—black still water, breaking up the horizon spanning tan saw grass clumps, occasionally sprouting a very lonely gray tree, all under a crystalline blue sky—lazed panoramically around them. Pink Floyd provided the musical score, crooning "Welcome my son … . Welcome to the machine … "

Bernie did not miss the irony.

"Bernie, there's not going to be a next time as far as this venture goes is there?" asked Saundra. "Isn't this the end of the road?"

"For this vein of inquiry, I'm afraid so," Bernie responded. A sigh, imperceptible to the casual listener, but keenly prevalent to his inner circle of friends (those in the minivan qualifying) hinted at his disappointment. He had been tracing the oral histories of the dozens of Native American tribes who may have been in Florida during Sabatez's debacle for the better part of a year, unearthing a myriad of interesting information on intertribal relations, but nothing even close to useful regarding the fate of Namor's kin. What was more frustrating was how much time he had burned in this failed venture. Unlike his historical work, stories did not have a specific location. There were no oral history libraries he could dig through. Finding stories meant finding old Indians who knew them. Finding old Indians was a spotty task involving a lot of driving, a lot of sitting around waiting, and a lot of listening … A LOT of listening.

Bernie had started with the assumption that the Sabatez account was accurate, and his thugs never set foot on land following the massive cannon barrage. They could never have massacred all the land tribe by merely firing artillery. There had to have been some survivors, perhaps quite a few. Bernie further proposed that with their village destroyed, and their attackers repelled but alive, Namor's land kin packed up and left, fearing the return of Sabatez or another like him. The conclusion question of this "If-Then" exercise therefore refined to:

Where did the land kin go?

The Spanish missions arriving in the 1530's found a thriving Timucuan community called Nocoroco when they reached Namor's (and hence Sabatez's) site, but the natives' appearance and customs resembled the Saint Johns tribes much more than those Sabatez described. Their records made no mention of the *homo aquaticus* genes, even when elaborating on their heathen customs. The priests kept excruciatingly detailed accounts. They wouldn't have missed that. Given this, Bernie was relatively certain that Nocoroco[1] inhabitants had no connection to Namor other than coincidental geography. His hunch was that the native survivors had plodded inland settling at some other desolate site, or they were absorbed by another tribe. He banked most of his expectations on the latter. In his studies, he had found that Florida Tribes were notoriously efficient at increasing their numbers by raiding and assimilating other tribes. Namor's kin, coming off a horrible battle, with all their belongings gone in flames, would have been relatively easy pickings. It was Bernie's hope that a tightly knit group would have kept their connection to their sea kin, if only through stories. And that they would send the stories down the generations, eventually, possibly, hopefully, to him.

This was a stretch, and everybody—especially Bernie—knew it, but his earlier stretch had produced Sabatez's journal, which, along with Bernie's analysis, was on its seventh printing, so the university granted him a wide berth.

Bernie and his assistants traveled from Louisiana to the Florida Keys via car, train, plane, canoe, airboat and hiking boot to document any story which might have remotely linked to Namor. Intricate legends of lost tribes, water spirits and sea gods poured into recording devices. They went anywhere that the possibility for a story led them: Living rooms, farms, retirement homes, hospices, tents, smoke infested breakfast dives, lodge halls, fishing piers, even the infamous tribe casinos and Bingo rooms. Sometimes to understand the speaker, they had to employ two or three translators to get from the specific elderly storyteller's dialect to English. Hundreds of spoken hours compiled as MP3s were run through voice recognition scrubbers generating the most elegant of paradoxes, a written chronicle of oral history. To the immense gratitude of the various tribal councils and historians alike, the university provided the recordings and text (in the Native and translated English voices) free on their website. For decades to come, scholars would benefit from this rich new source of material.

But Bernie wouldn't.

He had traced every lead to its dark, blind dead end. Nothing came close to useful. Plenty of others would benefit, and the stories were incredibly beautiful. For that he took solace, but his own personal haunts remained.

And, he had burned off another year. His relationship with Jane was comfortable, but stagnated. When together, they were … good, marvelous actually. She was literally everything he could have hoped for in a partner. They just weren't ever together. She definitely wanted to be more involved in his life. Bernie was pretty sure of that, especially when she told him, "Bernie, I want to be more involved in your life."

That clue was hard to miss.

Because his single-minded pursuit had no space for distractions, she had been the bond holding them together, cutting her work to the point of reprimand, squeezing a week end here and there for them between his Quixotic chases. When the stories finally tapered off, and Bernie found time to think about it, he felt like a jerk. A handicap of intelligence is being too smart to fool oneself. This kind, intelligent, funny, patient, not to mention quite attractive woman deserved better than what he was providing. So he granted her request, inviting her to participate in his "life," which this week end meant a romp into the Everglades to chat with a great grandfather visiting his Miccosukee family from South Dakota. The man was a Korean War Veteran, and had been a CPA, before retiring, so he was very "Americanized." There was a slim chance he'd have many tales of buckskins and tepees, but Bernie had been surprised before.

Saundra had also indicated in the same subtle manner of her mother that she too wanted to come. Had she not invited herself, he would have offered her a seat as well. Bernie had been truly touched when she announced her intention to not only attend UM, but to study his chosen field. Saundra impressed him, not just because of her academic and athletic accomplishments, nor because she was so amazingly and uniquely mature, and not even because she was the daughter of someone he dated. Not really. Bernie liked her because she had accepted his intrusion into their tight mother/daughter relationship so seamlessly. She had accepted his presence without the horrific tensions he had been warned about by friends.

Granted her father was a piece of work, but that had all the more adhered Saundra to Jane. She, by all accounts, should at least initially have been wary, sarcastic, even a bit passive aggressive, bordering on rude. But she wasn't. For that, Bernie owed her. And despite a bunch of promises he had initially made the day she revealed her career path; promises he had then every intention of keeping; he hadn't followed through. Saundra never complained, but he could tell she had been growing frustrated that he wasn't bringing her along when he did his oral history research runs. She did drop occasional hints of her usefulness;

"I can set up the equipment a *lot* better and quicker than you can dinosaur boy," she affirmed correctly.

"I'm cheap. You don't have to pay me, and I'll bring my own lunch," she added for emphasis.

"And I'm smaller and don't smell anywhere near as foul as your lug assistants," she stacked on.

Finally today he was doing right by her.

She and Nathan were inseparable, so the party grew to four. There were no other reliable leads to follow on this thought chain, so he might as well make the best of it. The three Ormond denizens drove down to Miami after work/school Friday night, crashing at Bernie's. The next morning, while they slept, he exchanged vehicles with a chemist who was moving his sister from a Miami Beach Condo to another Miami Beach Condo, grabbed some *pasteles* and *croquetas*[2] at the corner *bodega*[3] and met the gang early at his house. They mapped out their route, and made plans to catch a Marlins game that night.

" … ie?"

"Bernie?"

"Dr. Sherban!"

"Bernie! Over here. You went into your happy place again … How was your trip?" Saundra had a way of grounding Bernie.

"Yeah, sorry, miles away … I'm back now. What is it?" Bernie asked, reorienting himself to his surroundings.

"We're looking for the Miccosukee Village right?" Nathan asked.

"That's what the directions say."

"OK then. I think we need to turn around, 'cause I happened to read one of those brown info signs that said it's eight miles away."

"I don't understand—" Bernie began, but a quick glance at Nathan's reversed contorted position clarified the statement. Nathan was enjoying the view out of the rear window. Turning around on State Road 41, better known as Tamiami Trail was no small task. The eighty-eight mile section of the stretch of road that connected Tampa and Miami[4] cutting through the Everglades was essentially an elevated causeway surrounded by a three inch deep, slowly moving "River of Grass."

This deceptively large river, smeared across the entire south of the peninsula, transported Florida's waters from Lake Okeechobee, and the hundreds of Central Florida Springs into the Gulf of Mexico. The first two impressions the Everglades triggered were "vast" and "flat." With the exceptions of the occasional high ground consisting of a few scruffy trees desperately clinging here and there, and some haphazard pockets of standing water, an unbroken ocean of yellow brown grass, sopping wet at the base, stretched from horizon to horizon. There were no hills, forests, or other landmarks to block the field of sight. Limitations on how much Everglades a pair of eyes could see were set by the curvature of the Earth.

Humans had not been kind to this unique ecosystem. Urbanization had squeezed the smear into narrower and narrower paths; besides Tamiami, there was the smooth, divided four lane antiseptic I-75 route,[5] also clogging water flow. Cities, agriculture and industry had donated an exotic cocktail of waste products whose impact was only now being investigated as a massive clean up initiated in December of 2000[6] proceeds.

The Everglades was therefore not inclined to be very accommodating to humans, especially their vehicles. Trying to engage a three point turn on the narrow causeway with channels on both sides had over the years produced quite a few vertically shining headlights. Turning around was virtually impossible without some place to pull into ... and in the Everglades, there just weren't many places to do that.

They drove a ways, until finally something appeared on the north side of the road. A huge plywood sign with the words "Airboat Rides" spray painted in bright red and white cursive letters pointed to a small concrete block shack. There were no cars in the packed dirt parking lot. Bernie pulled in and spying a soda machine cut the engine. They all got out, and conducted their own versions of stretching their limbs. Saundra fished some change from her mother's purse and made for the soda machine.

"Who wants what?" she called out.

"Coke."

"Coke."

"Coke," came the replies.

While she performed her bartending duties, Bernie and Jane went around to the back of the building to see if anyone was there, and to find a bathroom. They came to another similarly written plywood sign pointing out into ... nowhere. Clearly, this sign once designated a destination, but much as they looked, they saw nothing in the grass and murky water.

"You here for a ride?" a crackly voice from inside the building asked.

"BATHROOM!" blurted Jane.

"Around the side. Door's open … Ain't very clean tho'," answered the voice.

Jane didn't hear anything after "around the side." Bernie shook his head in affectionate exasperation as he heard the door slam. He smiled. She always did that. Instead of asking for a restroom stop, Jane held it in so she wouldn't slow the trip down; choosing the inflated bladder torment over jibes that she was a typical, incontinent female. As usual, he chastised himself that he should have remembered from the last trip.

"So, you here for a ride?" the voice repeated.

"Ride? Oh, you mean, airboat. No, no thanks. We're just turning around, and grabbing some sodas." Bernie replied squinting into the shadowed porch trying to get a glimpse of the voice's originator.

"Good thing, 'cause I can't give you a ride anyways."

Bernie thought it peculiar that the advertised activity was unavailable.

"Airboat broke down?" he inquired, neighborly-like.

"Nope. Boat's fine. Just tuned it myself."

"Are you closed?"

"Nope."

"Out of fuel?"

"Nope"

Bernie's curiosity took over. "Do you want me to keep guessing or will you tell me what the problem is?"

"See the dock?" the voice asked.

Bernie turned back to the second sign. He saw a few loose boards, but beyond that nothing but grass.

"No. No I don't," Bernie conceded.

"That's why you can't get a ride."

"Dock got washed away? Which storm did it?"

"My sons and I build that dock. Ain't no storm goin' take it nowhere. Used good lumber and we anchored it with steel chains to some big boulders from a construction site near Krome.[7] Dock's *there* all right—about 200 feet in and ten feet down."

Creaking from wood and old joints emanated from the spot where the shadow's voice came. A cowboy stepped into the sunlight … or an Indian. Both really. Dressed in the garb of a rodeo man, well-worn, white ten-gallon hat with a frayed blue band sporting a pathetic excuse for a feather, blue checkered shirt with the long sleeves rolled up tightly at the bicep, thick worn-out jeans and some very exotic steel-tipped boots, a stocky, deeply-tanned elderly Native American stepped into the sunlight. His hair was shoulder length and silken white. Light skin where the sun never had a chance to activate the pigment cells peaked around the fringe of his arms and neck until he adjusted his attire to his new standing position. He was drinking a Coca-Cola. Despite months of interviewing for practice, Bernie had long ago surrendered any hope of guessing the age of men such as this. For the most part, they had lived hard lives, inordinately aging their bodies, yet at some point, the genetics of their race kicked in and their appearance reached a plateau. So the voice's owner could be fifty or he could be ninety.

"Seems a funny place to build a dock, but I guess if you put it there, you're right. Ain't no hurricane gonna take it."

The voice's owner crinkled, "It wasn't so funny when we put it up. The dock was really nice. A whole boatload could be standin' on it waitin' to board. Sturdy too, hardly any bounce, even when the college boys tried jumpin' all at once to scare the sorority girls. Took the storms like a wall. Didn't budge an inch … Then Naples and Miami started worryin' about their rainfall, and they closed a bunch of them flood gates. Kept their water lines low, but we rose a good eight to ten feet. Drowned my dock. Look in the water. Can you see it?"

Bernie scanned the murky depths, and he did indeed see the dock now. It was floating sideways about six feet below the surface, anchored firmly to the bottom by four boulders attached to chains. Pilon stumps were all that remained of the walkway to it.

"Insurance?" Bernie asked.

"Better'n that. BIA.[8] They paid us good for the dock, and my son moved his business to a site by the Miccosukee Village with a lot more traffic. We're doin' all right."

"You have no dock, or boat. Why are you here?" Bernie asked.

"Saw that soda machine out front? It's got a short in the wiring. Hold the three Coke buttons down and I can get a bottle ... I come here for the Cokes." And as if to emphasize this, the Cola Man chugged the remainder of his bottle and carefully set it in a recycling bin that contained dozens of other empty carefully set coke bottles.

"Time for another," he said, starting his way around to the front, adding, "Sometimes, I get some good conversation too."

The two men made their way to the street-side of the block structure. Cola Man, true to his word, pushed the three "Coke" buttons on the sun-bleached, rusty machine and, like a conjurer's rabbit, a coke plunked out of the proper opening.

"Don't they notice the loss of revenue?" Bernie asked.

"Well ya see, once a week there's this nice guy wearing a uniform who comes out along this road and empties the money from the machine. He talked to me for a while once. Says his company owns around a hundred of 'em, and his job is to gather the money and turn it in."

"Let me guess, and then *another* guy comes out to stock it." Bernie interjected.

Cola Man eyed Bernie for a moment, assessing whether he was in trouble because his crimes had been discovered. Bernie didn't know this, but Cola Man was assessing whether or nor Bernie was sent by the vending machine company as a spy. Finally, he reached a decision that Bernie was all right.

"You don't sound tourist. Are you a professor?"

This blunt, accurate observation took Bernie by surprise. "Yes. Yes I am. How'd you know that?"

"I ain't got no boat rides to give so I pass the time figuring folks out. Not too hard really, 'cause there ain't but a few types that come out this way anyway. Thought you were tourist first, 'cause you got that minivan and you ain't dressed proper for the heat and mosquitoes. But tourists ain't calm like you all. They're clumsy spastic, louder than they need to be, runnin' around snappin' photos of any fool thing they find. Most times, they never even realize I'm here. I just sit in the shadow and watch them pee in the river."

"You hide from tourists?"

"Can't give them a ride, so I can't take their money. I show my face and they take my picture with their whole family. My rockin' chair useta be out front before I got smart. I'm probably in three or four hundred family albums." At the thought of this, his smile broadened.

Still wincing from the minivan labeling, Bernie asked, "It's a big leap from non-tourist to professor."

"You ain't dressed for today, but you been here before … been here before, quite a bit. I reckon you're an expert on some plant, or bug, or something, that you've been studying for all your life, and it's only found here in our "Amazing River of Grass" and you're bringing your girlfriend and kids to see it on your day off … Am I right?"

"Sort of," Bernie admitted.

Nathan and Saundra came around the corner, each bearing two cokes in hand. A much relieved Jane joined them. She took her drink as well.

"What else besides tourist and professor could I have been?" Bernie asked.

"Artist" Cola Man answered. His mouth curled at the word as if it left an unpleasant flavor. "Them artistic types always comin' out here to be one with my people. They buy junk 'cause it's "Injun Junk." Some of them write in little journals. Some sketch. They talk loud, even cryin' sometimes about how horrible the US has treated us poor Indians, not because they really feel bad, but because they want folks to *know* that they really feel bad. I think they're convinced we have some deep secret we've kept from the white man … but we'll tell *them* because they won't wear a 'Noles T-shirt," and the old man started a laugh. It was a pleasant contagious roll that never broke the surface. But his whole body rumbled happily.

Bernie liked this guy.

"We have an appointment a few miles back to get to. It was very nice talking to you." Bernie said extending his hand.

"What appointment you got on a Saturday in the Everglades?" Cola Man queried, returning the handshake.

Bernie gave Cola Man an abridged version of his work, and the circumstances which brought them to his submerged dock and soda machine. The old man quietly absorbed the narrative, occasionally sipping his drink as Bernie spoke, uninterrupted, from Namor's discovery through Sabatez, and to this morning's drive. A lengthy silence followed. The minivan party could tell Cola Man had something he was working out in his mind, and granted him the courtesy of the quiet to assemble it.

After an indeterminate silence, Cola Man spoke." I got a story for ya."

This was unexpected.

"You sure?" Bernie asked somewhat skeptically.

"Pretty sure … Pretty darned sure," Cola Man emphasized. "I got some Calusa in me. My grandmother had even more. She useta tell me lotsa stories that her grandmother had told her 'bout the great Sea Spirit Talimiqua. That it was watchin' over us when we went in the water. My grandmother's grandmother was livin' out here with her family since the dawn of time the way she tells it, then them Northern Injuns, Muskogee, Seminole, other folks, came bargin' into her swamp pushed down here by the white man. She'd probably have killed them all if she hadn't fallen in love. Married a Seminole man and we've been on the reservation since. But grandmother's grandmother was wild. No doubt about it."

"Your grandmother's grandmother was a Spanish Indian?" Bernie declared astonished.

"Think so," affirmed Cola Man.

Nathan couldn't hold himself back any longer.

"What's a Spanish Indian?"

"Spanish Missions flooded into Florida in the 1500's—" Bernie began.

"Looking for Namor's people right?" Nathan interjected.

"We don't know that. Their journals indicated they were introducing Christianity to the New World ..."

"And smallpox, and slavery, and war ... " Nathan added.

Bernie had seen Nathan wind up like this before. Once in full passion mode, he'd be impossible to stop and Bernie really wanted to hear Cola Man's story. With a quick eye and hand gesture, he signaled for Saundra to cut him off.

"And they decimated most of the indigenous tribes including the Calusa-mmmrmmmffff!"

Saundra's smothering kiss immediately derailed her boyfriend's train of thought.

"As I was saying, Nathan," Bernie continued, "the Spaniards were here long enough that, by 1700, most Calusa people spoke their language. That's about the time that the tribes disappeared altogether, done in by that cheerful "hat trick" of destruction you were so enthusiastically preaching about. A few escaped the Spaniards temporarily by migrating to Cuba. There were rumblings that some headed deep inland, disappearing into the wild. It's one of those Urban Legends or, in this case, Very Rural Legends, that some pockets of Spanish-speaking, Calusa descendants still live out in the Everglades today."

Saundra stopped kissing Nathan long enough for him to breathlessly thank Bernie for the history lesson. He was about to reengage his girlfriend when Jane stepped between them.

"I read about your skeleton up North and thought about them stories, but I figured everyone had a water spirit legend here and there," said the Cola Man.

Bernie's was intrigued. His interest level amplified significantly as soon as Cola Man mentioned the Calusa link. That Southwest Florida tribe was infamous for its marauding. They were seafarers and fishermen, and physically similar to the Timucuan. It was a small leap, indeed, to consider that the remaining Calusa tribe members had absorbed Namor's land kin. Bernie had already banked many interviews with men and women linked ancestrally to the Calusa. Their stories were mostly nautical in theme, but as disjointed to one another as would be expected from a loosely arranged culture.

"You got a particular story in mind?" Bernie asked.

"Yeah, I think I do," confirmed the Cola Man. "There was one about a baby she useta tell us, I think you'll like. She was tryin' to get us appreciatin' how much our Moms were sacrificin' for us, but we just liked it 'cause it was a good story and she squeezed us orange juice to drink while she told it."

"Mind putting that story on the record?" Bernie asked.

"Nope."

"Saundra, why don't you and Nathan set the recording equipment up around back, somewhere in the shade?"

Bernie introduced Jane, and the three adults made small talk as the kids set up the improvised studio.

True to her word, Saundra had everything running in a fraction of the time Bernie would have. Cola Man grabbed another free drink, made a pit stop in the filthy restroom, and sat down in his rocker. Nathan pinned the pickup microphone to his shirt and, a sound check later, narrating to a mesmerized audience of four, the Cola Man began.

"The way this story goes is this … "

CHAPTER
10

The
Cola Man's Story

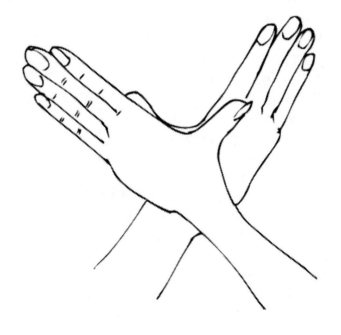

Skin Mender groaned softly as she slashed away at the wet underbrush. Her tiny hatchet swung furiously, waging a futile war with the dense forest. Countless cuts marking the forest's dominance of the battle oozed a drop or two each … Insignificant alone, together they blended with the dirt and leaves to tint her body crimson. Another birth pain jarred her, and this time she nearly doubled over. Her sudden lurch wedged the hatchet between two branches. She clutched at it tightly until the pain diminished. A deep breath later, she was on her way again. A glint of a smile creased her lips.

Talamiqua had not seen her buckle.

She heard waves crashing. Strengthened by the sound of her journey's end, she accelerated her pace.

"One hundred trees—" she estimated, "One hundred trees away, my child will hear the Birth Song."

Her thoughts wandered to Wind Arrow. She cursed him in her mind. How dare he claim that he would have wanted to accompany her if the Ways permitted! She imagined he was probably sitting in the shade against the Council House with his companions, sharpening his favorite spear the way he always did on such hot days.

"I would like to do something else with that spear of yours, my precious little husband!" she grumbled.

Instantly she took her words back. Wind Arrow was truly a good man. He was kind and respected. His talent at finding meat was in her eyes better than his father's (who the Tribe claimed was the greatest hunter that ever served them). Wind Arrow knew duty. He never returned with empty hands. He would gladly have accompanied her but he dared not. Too many omens had cast a shadow on their child already.

If only they had not saved the girl mauled by the great fish. But what were they to have done? The attack occurred at the shore early in the morning. It was a desperate shark that had wandered too far into the river. The sweeter waters were slowly killing it, and it was mad with pain and hunger. Both she and Wind Arrow were witnesses. He always walked her down to the nets, especially so since she carried his child. From the moment he heard the scream, Wind Arrow did not hesitate. He never did. Three arrows sank deep into the beast's snout, then Wind Arrow jumped at it. The combination of pain and impact dislodged the girl ... Wind Arrow carried her to the bank and the beast swam off, never to be seen again.

Her wounds were severe. Skin Mender feared Wind Arrow's bravery was for nothing, but she was as good a mender as her husband was a hunter. She aggressively tended the wounds. Clean salt water brought by Wind Arrow gushed the skin gapes, flushing the blood away so she could see the depth of the damage. A bitter salve ground from palm roots temporarily dammed the bleeding and, with thin fish bones, she began sealing the many cuts before the root's magic wore off.

Even as she performed her art, the reprisals began.

"It was her fate to quiet the beast's raging hunger—" the Tribe complained.

"Best we return her to the water quickly so it may finish its meal."

Skin Mender evoked her privilege as Mender and ignored the voices of omen. The little girl survived, but would be crippled. The girl's family had five other children and was unwilling to accept the burden of providing for her, so she belonged to Skin Mender's family now. They had been blamed for every mishap since.

"A god denied his pleasure will not rest until avenged," accused Soaring Spear at the last Council House Fire Talk. He spoke with bitterness. There was little rain this season, and the hunting was scarce. His anger sought causes where there were none, so it sought excuses. The words he bellowed as his wife led him away echoed in her head, "Talamiqua will take your child to feed the great fish! He will never let you deny his pet ... Never!"

Skin Mender could not remember how many nights she had laid awake terrified of Soaring Arrow's prophecy. Her fears were shared by most of the Tribe. The women gossiped that her daughter (Dancing Eyes' had visioned a girl) may already be dead. Wind Arrow dismissed the gossip.

"Feel the punches and kicks my wife," he would say, slowly stroking her belly. "Our daughter shows more life than most of the Tribe children, and she is still imprisoned within you. It would be wise for you to put these gossips aside and rest now. You will get little of it when she comes out."

Skin Mender would pretend to feel better so her husband would stop worrying. But does not a dying animal also writhe violently in the pain of death?

The trees thinned, and eventually gave way to sand and shell. Skin Mender was at the shore. Raw sunlight pierced her eyes, ripping away her day dreams. After being wet so long, her body welcomed the warmth. She let it seep into her and bake off the shivering.

This proved a mistake. She had forgotten how grimy she was. The caked forest litter and blood attacked her with an unbearable itch as they dried. She knew scratching would only worsen the problem. Relief would only come from the water, so she continued her walk.

Moving in short, shuffly steps to keep her feet under the hot white surface sand, when she at last reached the water, she felt the first real temptation to collapse.

"Not now," she struggled within herself, "Especially not at Talamiqua's doorstep. He will surely take her if I fail now."

With a silent scream only she would ever hear, Skin Mender went to work. She found a cool spot just out of reach of the waves and made her Birth Bed.

"It must face Talamiqua's realm," her mother had instructed. "Better to dig down so that you can gather cool sand, than to pile it up. And daughter ... Never forget the Sign of the Tail."

Molding the bed was not as difficult as she expected. The sand was soft and loosely packed, yielding easily to any form she molded. Skin Mender's daughter assisted by remaining mercifully still throughout her task.

She rose and examined her Birth Bed. It met her mother's strict instructions nicely and, to her delight, looked quite comfortable. Just after she stood, a deep wrenching pang gripped her. A reminder from her daughter that there was still work to do.

"You are as impatient as your father," she groaned, waiting for the pain to pass.

Skin Mender turned to the water. She raised her arms slowly, forming the sacred gesture of worship of the women of her Tribe. Arms stretched straight up, the back of her left hand pressed to the palm of the right, fingers of each hand parallel and touching, opposing thumbs aligned to fit the finger contours.

Skin Mender swayed the perfectly formed Sign of the Tail, back and forth until she felt satisfied that Talamiqua saw it. Her salute concluded, she took one last pause to organize her thoughts, and with a few steps, abandoned the white heat of her world to enter the dark biting cold of Talamiqua's.

Salty water gushed around her expelling the sunlight from her cuts. It purified her skin, purging the dirtiness of her pilgrimage as fire purged flesh from bone. Mercifully, Talamiqua numbed her with the cold. She suffered a little, but was relieved to have the itching leave. Skin Mender waded until she was waist deep between waves, repeated the Sign and began her Birth Song. She sang quietly at first. The Birth Song had always been taught secretly from mother to daughter, leaking just a fragment to a man was unthinkable. Even accidental eavesdropping by a husband or a son would be disastrous to the Tribe. She had therefore never sung it in a voice louder than the most breathless of whispers.

Her ears were not accustomed to hearing it so clearly, and it made her feel giddy. She braved a quick glance around to reassure her seclusion. Once consoled, a mischievous beam cracked her lips, and she raised her voice slightly. She found herself giggling at this new volume and raised her voice even more. A large wave would occasionally drown her out, but she would surface singing even louder and laughing more vigorously than before. It was the familiar laughter of childish disobedience, and she relished it.

Birth pains shrilled her voice at times, giggling squeaked it, and the crashing waves sometimes muffled the Birth Song, but Skin Mender finished it. With a hoarse voice, she thanked Talamiqua for listening, made the Tail Sign one last time, and returned to her Birth Bed. She fell into it in as dignified a manner as she could manage and prepared for the ordeal she knew was about to unfold.

Birth pains attacked and retreated with increasing frequency. Occasionally, she would still be reeling from one when another would hit. By the time the sun had changed the direction of shadows, there were no intervals. She was in the Final Pain.

Skin Mender dug her heels into the sand. Deep grooves formed, tracing the path of her motions. She clutched tightly at the woven cloth made by her mother she had brought along for drying the baby. It was a tight pattern of two moss strands over and three under which no one else in the Tribe used, nor most likely, would ever use. The time involved in weaving it was too great. The completed cloths could dry, warm, and clean. They met their limit however, with this task. Knuckles whitened, her fists vibrated fiercely from the intensity of her grip on the rapidly shredding garment.

"Talamiqua! Feel my suffering!" she cried out, "Feel how I gladly cherish the pain for my child. Let your great beast feed on the many fishes you have made for him!"

She gathered her strength and pushed. Reaching down between her legs, she felt a head. Again she pushed, and felt a nose. Another push revealed lips and a shoulder. Several pushes later, seizing the tiny arms which emerged, and her last bits of energy, Skin Mender freed her baby from her womb.

Drained of all strength, she lost her grip, and the baby fell to the sand. Skin Mender lay breathless and nervous. When some air returned, she propped herself on her elbows, and gingerly scooted to a seated position.

She stared at the water.

"Talamiqua please ..." she pleaded softly, and looked at her child. Horror realized cuts deeper than horror imagined. Skin Mender was overwhelmed by the creature she birthed and tore her gaze away. But even with closed eyes, the vision of the creature she had been carrying and suffering for, burned itself in her mind and would never be removed. Soaring Spear was wrong, but his prophecy would have been more welcome than this. A garbled, high pitched sound rose from the thing Skin Mender's Womb ejected. She tried to ignore it.

"This is not my baby," she sobbed to herself, an aching pain pushing on the back of her throat. "I will have no pity for it. Let it suffer as Wind Arrow and I will suffer." But the sound would not stop. She pushed her hands over her ears and squeezed her eyes shut. She tried desperately to seal herself up, but the sound seeped in between her fingers. It entered her mind and lodged itself firmly, demanding her attention. She felt her hands fall to her sides, her eyes soften, her body unclench. The sound disarmed her. Again she sat up, and again gazed at what she had birthed.

The creature's face was normal. She even had to admit it was quite pleasant. Thick black hair crowned wide blue eyes, a slender perfect nose and mouth. The arms, although unnaturally strong for an infant, and the hands a bit larger than expected, were also relatively normal. The upper torso, she concluded, was of the Tribe, and quite beautiful.

But the creature had two halves.

Deep fissures ran along the gaps between its lower ribs. A fleshy flap covered them. Without it, there was no doubt that she would have had a clear view of its lungs. The flaps opened and closed in rhythm with its chest. She found a barely visible skin sac, where one would ordinarily look to determine the gender of a child. Skin Mender touched it softly. She felt nothing of note to indicate a male, verifying the predictions of Dancing Eyes.

The creature had no legs. Or rather, it appeared as if it had legs once, but all the body from the pelvis downward had somehow been softened to clay and molded into something else. It had but one lower limb. The muscles of that single limb were thick and sturdy. There was no knee. Rather, the entire lower limb bent like a new branch. A tiny protrusion jutted from where it should have had calves, and it writhed in directions impossible for Tribe bones to turn. At the base, where she expected to find heels, she instead discovered a tight lump. The feet, flattened grotesquely, jutted out from the lump, Yet they still divulged their origins. Five ridges marked where the bones ran through.

The sounds she was hearing originated at the rib fissures. Meek whistles escaped from each slit as the thing's chest heaved. Small bubbles foamed their fringes. She saw the mouth gasping silently for breath, but failing miserably to acquire it. The creature was dying.

Throughout its ordeal, its eyes were riveted on her.

"I ... We did not cause this," she sobbed in response to the stare. "Our only failure was relieving pain and preventing death from snatching one who did not deserve such a fate." She turned towards the ocean.

"What god can punish kindness?" she cried out defiantly.

The creature only stared. Its skin was now a bluish tinge. Skin Mender had seen this color before. It was the shade of water victims. Talamiqua had indeed claimed her child. The realization tightened her torso. Her contortion expelled the last of the after-birth on the creature's face. She thought of leaving it there to clip the suffering, but decided that cheating even a moment of life, however wretched, was for a god to decide and she had no intention of starting another quarrel. She cleared her daughter's face of the slick wet chunk they had both shared for so long. When she wiped off the blood with her mother's cloth, the skin appeared slightly less blue.

"Most likely you are still blue," she said sharply. The back of her throat aching even more, "And the muck on you prevents me from seeing it. In any event creature, Talamiqua has claimed you. I cannot bicker."

Skin Mender carefully scooped up her child. "Oh, but you might have been so beautiful," she thought, gazing at the face. She tied off the umbilical a fist away from the creature's belly, and sliced off the bulk with one quick bite. She tried to stand, but stumbled. Innately, she rolled on her back as she fell so that her child would not come to harm. Seated on the scorching white sand, bombarded by the relentless heat of the sun, she found herself trembling. She began to cry an uncontrolled lament for a child too soon taken away.

"Talamiqua it is not right!" She bawled as she stood again. Sobbing loudly, and with wobbly steps, she entered Talamiqua's realm a second time, maneuvering to about the same depth she had been before. Skin Mender raised her daughter to her face. She was barely moving but still conscious.

Her blue eyes hollowed, but still open, she gazed sleepily at her mother. Skin Mender kissed her child on the nose. "Good bye creature. Good bye my daughter," she whispered. Gently she lowered her below the waves and relaxed her grip. The infant sank quickly away from her. When the next wave waned, she was alone.

A rage simmering inside her grumbled its desire for freedom. Slowly at first, then erupting with a vengeance, her rage boiled. She scanned the horizon intensely, seeking the cruel god who cheated her. Her entire body ached from the travel and the birth. Her cuts stung, deep wrinkles from the water, and bumps from the cold deformed her skin, but these were matters of little importance. She wanted Talamiqua.

"I am here coward!" She challenged, "Show yourself. Show me the cowardly god who punishes those who defy him by killing their children. Show me so that I may see the face of this monster!" She punched at the approaching waves fiercely. When she was too tired to continue, she churned the waters around her, all the while screaming her challenge and taunting. Filth cluttering her soul since childhood spilled into the waters. Every fear she ever felt, she blamed Talamiqua; every curse she heard, she flung at Talamiqua; every taunt, every cut, bruise, insult, and suffering she had ever felt, she wished on Talamiqua.

She maintained the frenzy until she was drained of both strength and emotion. The cold ocean waters again had cleansed her, but this time, they were more thorough. With her head bowed, she backed away to more shallow waters and sank to her knees. Only her head remained above the water. She was contemplating on whether she should lower herself to join her child when a man appeared in the water in front of her.

Although she did not recognize him, he was unquestionably of the Tribe. His face bore the stern chiseled features of her people, but she did not recognize him. His hair was thick and dark pulled back behind his head and held there by running it through a ring which was cut from a white shell. His skin was peculiarly tanned. His face and chest were pale, the hue of newborns and elders who confined themselves to their huts, but his back was quite dark. She deduced that he spent quite a lot of time on his belly. She could not determine how tall he was because he approached her from the water. When she turned around to check the sand to see from where he came, she saw her tracks, but no others.

The man smiled.

He reached to touch her face but she winced. In response, he held out his hand for her to take. When this too brought no response he made the Sign of the Tail, and arched his body back so that he floated face up on the surface.

Skin Mender muffled a scream. She was looking upon an adult whose features matched her daughter. He too was part Tribe, and part other. His chest and arms were strong, although she noted they were slightly less sinewy than Wind Arrow and the other Tribe men. A muscular abdomen creased his body from below his chest to the sac encasing his privates. The fissures along his ribs were deeper than her daughter's, even accounting for its greater size, and they had no flaps. Tiny, long healed scars lining both sides on the openings between the lower ribs hinted that this distinction might be unnatural.

Below the ribcage, his legs were smoothly sculpted into a powerful tail. She noticed quite a few nicks on the bony lump at the base. She imagined what a formidable weapon it would make. The flukes were thick, the toes she noted on her daughter hidden under thick muscle, and a sharp edge ran from tip to tip, skipping over the stump.

Skin Mender touched the man. He felt warm. She examined him with her fingers. She felt the deep chest expand and contract like hers would if she was to run a great distance. She felt strong currents of water rhythmically squirting from the fissures. She wondered where the water was entering, when she noticed, he had his head submerged by tilting it back. Moving down the torso, she discovered the protrusion just above his tail. More prominent in an adult, and obviously a fin, she found a second larger fin at his midback. Her hands continued the inspection, studying every part of the miraculous body. He endured the probes patiently. When she removed her hands, he disappeared.

He was gone for a short time. When he returned, he was not alone. A woman like him emerged at his side. She too had Tribe features, and the fissures. She was not particularly interesting in her Tribe portion, except for her eyes. Like the man and her daughter, they too were blue.

Skin Mender guessed the woman had a tail, but she could not see it. As the woman approached, it became clear that she was carrying her daughter. Her baby squirmed happily in the woman's arms. Her color was healthy, and she was breathing comfortably under the water. She fidgeted more actively than any newborn she had ever seen, her tiny body straining against the gentle but firm grip of the woman. Her efforts waxing and waning as fatigue and boredom set in and out of her new mind. Skin Mender extended her arms towards the woman. The woman smiled and handed over her baby.

Skin Mender gleefully raised her child to kiss her, but the infant immediately started choking, and the man nudged her hands down. Not to be cheated, she plunged below the water herself, and poured as much affection as her breath could withstand. She remained there, ignoring her burning lungs and stinging eyes, her exhaustion, the cold, the currents, and basked in the presence of the life she had produced. Eventually, gasping but happy, she broke the surface. The baby squirmed loose, swam clumsily to the woman, and snuggled in her arms. The woman looked apologetic as she smiled good bye and sank out of sight with the child. She continued staring at the spot where they dove until the man attracted her attention. He too had something in his arms.

It was a woven cloth for cleaning babies. The color was much faded, but there was no doubt of the stitching—it was a tight pattern of two strands over and three under which no one else in the Tribe used, nor most likely would ever use.

The man placed the cloth in her hand, took the one she brought, which was draped over her shoulder, and disappeared. Skin Mender went ashore. She collapsed on the sand, deciding that it would be better for her to spend the night here and return the next morning.

"Wind Arrow will worry," she thought. "No matter, I will explain it all to him." She laughed even as she thought the words. With her mother's cloth as a pillow, she drifted into a peaceful sleep.

That night, she dreamt she was a dolphin.

✳✳✳

Bernie cancelled his appointment that afternoon. They never made it to the Marlins game. For the rest of the day, he grilled Cola Man, recording every thought, memory, story, and rumor the old man remembered. Cola Man enjoyed nearly every minute of it. The one part neither was too keen on was when Bernie tried tracing events to someone else who might remember some more. Cola Man was the oldest and last living of three brothers. His siblings had many children, but they were completely "Americanized," living in Chicago and Pittsburgh, those types of places. Only he had retained any semblance of his heritage. Cola Man himself had two sons, both living nearby. Bernie spoke with both of them when they pulled up to collect their father at the end of the day. They were friendly enough, and promised to think about it, but they didn't sound very confident. They loved their father, that was obvious, but as in most tribes, it was their mother who had died three years ago whose lore they recalled.

Nathan and Saundra packed the equipment. The sons packed their father, and each vehicle set out in opposite directions on Tamiami.

Conversation in the minivan was lively. It was Saundra's turn to play the music, so with RadioHead in the background, Jane and Bernie discussed how they would approach the park service to expand their search for *Homo aquaticus* to the West Coast. Nathan asked Bernie how he felt about the good luck they just experienced in finding Cola Man.

"If you hadn't been in a zone, we wouldn't have missed the turn, and this day would have ended a lot differently. Man that is seriously lucky, almost too lucky really."

Bernie acknowledged the appearance of luck, but he reminded Nathan that the search for stories had been ongoing for nearly a year with negligible results. When broadened beyond the confines of this day, luck was statistically eliminated.

"We had amazingly good fortune today, I'll agree. But, by its very nature, we'll never know how much "bad luck" we've endured. How many times did we stand in line at a reservation check-out counter right next to someone else with an even better tale to tell? Or pump gas by the daughter of a Spanish Indian? Or asked the wrong question and missed a promising line of query? It's unfair to compare *visible* good fortune to *phantom* bad. I don't know who said it, but I'm positive it's true—Luck is where opportunity meets preparation. We were actively hunting for stories linking Native American Lore to Namor, and after a long year of labor, we found it. That's hard work Nathan, not luck," Bernie said.

"The fact is that the only real "luck" was that the three of you were present when we found this story," he concluded.

With that, the subject changed to an animated debate over which Disney Cartoon was the most finely scripted (Nathan choosing *Toy Story* and Bernie *The Lion King,* with Jane and Saundra chiming in on the side of *Mulan)* They freshened up at Bernie's while he set the voice scrubbers to transcribe Cola Man's wonderful narrative, and they all celebrated at a very nice restaurant. Throughout the trip and meal, Saundra drifted in and out of the chatter. A thought was nagging at her that was too silly to really bring up, but it just wouldn't go away. She eventually dropped it, and leapt into the celebration. But chiseled permanently in the stone of Saundra's "To Do" list, to be resolved to her satisfaction someday, was finding a definitive answer to a simple question;

"Which Calusa opted to go to Cuba?"

CHAPTER
11

Aquatiacs

The University of Miami's *Homo Aquaticus* Discovery Center at Tomoka State Park opened with the extraordinary fanfare usually reserved for Vegas Casinos and Hollywood Blockbusters.

That wasn't what the curators intended.

Their vision was a modest, solemn procession marking the return of Namor's remains to their resting place, a speech or two by someone with enough clout to coax a few TV stations' camera crews, and an open house with free bagels and coffee so folks could snack as they got a peak at the exhibits.

Things simply got out of hand.

The politicians started it. Invitations were sent to pretty much everyone remotely connected to Florida's government on the off chance one or two would agree to come. Recognizing an important "schmoozing" opportunity ALL of them had enthusiastically RSVP'd that they would be happy to attend. So officials spanning the gamut of the state's electoral food chain starting with the governor and both US Senators, cascading down through the house and senate, all the way to Ormond's mayor and school principals were here. They were joined by colleagues from other states who were easily identifiable in their sweat-darkened power suits, bloated with gallons of the wearer's fluids.

Unlike the Floridians (and those visitors smart enough to check the weather or ask around *before* packing for the trip) these men and women from the cooler clines suffered the Catch-Twenty-Two[1] of whether to endure their jacket (which looked so good on them at the hotel) exacerbating the discomfort, or remove it and thus exposing their drenched sticky clothing underneath. Style over logic ruling their decisions this day, most chose the former so they worked the crowds shaking hands and kissing babies, while their pores performed the service of a sprinkler system in their clothing. They had to keep moving because puddles sometimes formed if they stayed still too long.

This cacophony of important policy makers drew the attention of the news media. They all sent crews to chronicle both the event and the politicians.

The media then attracted a freak show featuring many, many, MANY celebrities. Outnumbering the politicians nearly two to one, they strutted and primped outrageously jostling for camera time. Two major motion picture studios were making film versions of Sabatez's journal and they all wanted to be the first to quell the rumors that they so desperately hoped existed about their involvement in them.

But the "beautiful people" were incidental to the unfolding pageant, a mere blip on the RADAR[2] when compared to the throngs of interested civilians. Tens of thousands of said throngs having congregated for the event, inundating the already burgeoning hotels and campgrounds from Jacksonville to Orlando at the peak of their busy season. If the collage of license plates (every continental state and even a few unexplainable Hawaii tags) and the multitude of languages and accents were any indication, the throng came from literally everywhere.

They poured into the park, forcing the rangers to close the gates after every possible chunk of dirt that could hold a car was taken. Cars were still stacked to get in, so the Florida Highway Patrol had to close Old Kings Road, creating a makeshift parking lot on the shoulder. Denied their vehicles, the throng took to the road on bikes, skates, and foot. Others came along the river, either up the Tomoka or from the intercoastal, forming an eclectic flotilla off the park's banks that kept the Coast Guard as busy as the state troopers.

As was stated earlier … things got out of hand.

Tomoka's tree canopy blocked accurate aerial crowd estimates, but the guesswork *started* with one hundred thousand. The curators had woefully underestimated the expected size of the crowd.

They had budgeted enough bagels for two hundred.

Their monumental miscalculation was understandable. These were not dumb people. They were academic purists working diligently to get a facility presentable by a deadline. Reams of literature had to be evaluated; more reams of paperwork had to be completed. Their days were spent in the realm of permits, inspectors, staffing, inventory, construction, funding, and the odd custodial chore. It was happy but exhausting work. As such, they did not waste much time engaged in frivolous activities such as watching TV or thumbing magazines. They had therefore completely missed American Pop Culture's growing obsession with *Homo aquaticus* until its fans literally stormed their buildings by land and sea.

If just one of them had been lazy, or had at least poked their head out of their closed environment to get some air, they would have easily noticed the gathering mob. The embers of this phenomenon took a while to ignite, but, stoked with Sabatez's journal, Cola Man's published story (romantically titled "The Tale of Talimiqua"), along with a string of secondary publications hypothesizing on more subtle conjecture derived from Bernie's data such as Namor's top swimming speed, diet, habitat, temperature and depth tolerance, it had exploded into an uncontrolled information wildfire.

In accordance with the unwritten rules of these phenomena, those first obsessed created dozens of web pages, chat rooms, and blogs, dedicated to disseminating all *aquaticus* knowledge—from the biblically true and verified to rampant gossip. These sites not only provided fodder for perpetuating the maniacal following, but they were excellent for the casually interested to easily acquire information, thus creating more obsessed fans, who then sprouted more sites, etc.

The cycle steadily churned out "Aquatiacs"[3] until there were sufficient numbers to attract the "mainstream" media. Educational cable channels jumped in first. Discovery Channel, PBS, even Animal Planet and Nickelodeon ran specials on Namor and his species. CNN and Fox, in their talking head shows, discussed both the

Aquatiac craze and the ramifications of the species in human history. HBO and Cartoon Network both announced animated series with *Homo aquaticus* characters.

Once TV jumped in, the metaphorical barn doors were blasted wide open, and the fad ran amok.

A shame that the curators missed it all, especially since this wasn't by any means, the typical craze.

Working on the age old premise that wanting a thing was an infinitely more powerful urge than actually having the thing, traditionally nationwide obsessions were all about illusions. The latest movie or show or song or toy or car or fashion was an attempt by its marketers to create an allure which could only be acquired by viewing, or owning whatever it was they peddled. It wasn't the product itself that they sold, but the illusion of that product.

And since illusions were so enticing, and ownership so hollow, there was always a market for illusions. How else could untalented teenage boys and girls sell a million CDs? Why else would anyone buy a car that can go over 100mph in a country that won't let you go over 70 anywhere? Who would pay MORE money for LESS comfortable clothing? And could there be another rationale for the tradition of clearing out a child's closet of the "must have" toys from LAST Christmas to make room for the "must have" toys of THIS Christmas?

Clearly the purchasers were buying the illusions. The untalented teens who gazed longingly at the cameras in their music videos really made a connection that would perhaps tighten if the viewer bought their CD ... It didn't. The fast car was going to make such a bold statement about the driver's virility; he (or she) would have to fight off suitors with sticks ... But it just guzzled gas, and broke down a lot. The uncomfortable clothes would make the wearer as beautiful as the anorexic supermodel who hyped them ... They didn't. And no one ever had as much fun using a toy as the maniacally happy cheerful actors who played with them on the commercial.

The illusions disappeared the moment they become real. People complained they were cheated, and moved on to the next illusion.

Ebay servers are crammed with a graveyard of failed illusions. Namor was different. He was not an illusion. He was real. His very existence instantly connected all humans to a larger picture. Learning about Namor elevated rather than severed the connection. No corporation was working to conjure up the latest Namor accessories, or a *Homo aquaticus* video game. And if they were, their efforts were futile. T-shirts, pins, caps, trading cards, and toys had already flooded the market. No one was buying.

Rather than spending frivolously on merchandise, people were taking courses in oceanography. Public libraries were overwhelmed with requests for references on Florida's Native Americans, and marine biology. Beach attendance soared. Folks were strolling on the shore, looking to the sea more meaningfully. Aquatiacs up and down the coast took to standing watch on the ocean ... hoping. Marine park admissions skyrocketed.

All this information unfortunately escaped the notice of the hard working, but clueless, curators. Had they known, the unfolding circus would still have occurred. It would just have been less frazzling.

Finally, after an eternity in the hot sun, the opening ceremonies began at the river's shore with the unveiling of a monument erected on Namor's burial site. Over an inadequate sound system pointed at both the land and river crowds, and simulcast by CNN and Fox News (which had preempted their lineups) the head curator, a dapper older gentleman tapped from the Smithsonian's Natural History Museum stepped up to the podium and, declaring the statue would serve as both a tomb and a beacon, unveiled it to the clamor of ship's horns and roaring applause.

Then, in an impressive show of reverence, the crowds stilled as Namor's bones were reinterred. Manuel Gomez and dignitaries of the various Florida Tribes emerged from one of the center's buildings, and acting as pallbearers, carried Namor down the boardwalk to the opening at the monument's base. Only the sounds of buffoon news people under the delusion that their commentary would add to the scene broke the silence, and even they shut down after noticing the nasty glares.

Namor was transferred into the airtight chamber below the statue, and the door was sealed.

More applause. More blares.

A handful of others gave very brief speeches, making jokes about the same things—crowd size and the heat—then the University of Miami's *Homo Aquaticus* Discovery Center threw its doors open to the mob. Aquatiacs mingled freely with the politicians and the freaks, as they explored the three-story complex dedicated to collecting, analyzing and displaying *Homo aquaticus* information.

It was a rather expansive, aesthetically pleasing, but unassuming structure. Five interlocked buildings, each housing a specific theme followed the contours of the Tomoka River, arranged to exploit the natural breezes and lighting. Center patrons had the run of the first two levels, (the top floor housing offices and laboratories was unavailable to the general public.) An interesting curiosity of most of the exhibits was the tense. Rather than emphasizing history, the center focused on either the "now" or the future. There was a Native American wing, for example, that briefly described the migration of the various tribes throughout Florida, but the primary focus was on their current status. Touch screens also granted access to the terabytes of recorded oral histories—particularly Cola Man's tale.

Touchable moldings of Namor's skeleton and many manipulative displays explaining the dynamics of how his anatomy and physiology might have functioned filled another wing. Oceanography, Marine Biology, and current research avenues rounded out the sets of exhibits. Visitors also had the opportunity to explore Tomoka State Park. As the likely home of the tribe Namor defended, wandering through the largely pristine oak canopy where some of the trees may have been around at the time of Sabatez's attack added an even deeper experience.

A line to Namor's monument formed. People filed along, waiting patiently for the opportunity to simply touch the tomb. Sensing that this was not enough, but ignorant of what else to do, they were leaving flowers, or a drawing made by a child, or a poem they themselves had written. One man changed all that. A concrete sales-man from Jacksonville named Eddy who didn't really care for the whole Aquatiac phenomena, but drove here because his two young daughters had read the sanitized picture book of Sabatez's journal and they really REALLY wanted to come, made a simple, elegant gesture that became the ultimate sign of respect to be forever re-peated at Namor's grave.

The girls had noticed all the flowers and letters piling up at the tomb, and were feeling a bit sad that they had nothing to give Namor. Eddy, who had missed the preseason Jaguars game *and* drove sev-eral hours through traffic *then* walked about two miles because that's the closest he could get his car, JUST for the privilege of waiting in the blazing Florida sun for this chance was NOT going to leave his daughters with a bad memory after his investment.

Thinking fast, he remembered they had been talking about why Sabatez was so mean. The girls could not understand why Sabatez would hurt Namor when all Namor wanted to do was give him water. Eddy had explained to them that Sabatez was a bad guy and he was ungrateful for the gift. When he reached the front, he opened his bottled water and told the girls; "Let's give Namor back the water" and poured out a sip, thus symbolically returning the water the ungrateful Sabatez squandered. He handed the bottle to his girls who each poured out a sip, and they left happily to see some more things. A woman, three people back, heard Eddy and repeated the gesture, as did three men, further down the line, and five chil-dren afterwards. Soon everyone in line had water with them. A ritual evolved. The person at the front would touch the tomb with one hand, and pour a sip of water with the other.

Eddy never gave his gesture another thought. His idea served its purpose.

Thus traditions are born.

The crowds were enormous. The center overwhelmed, but other than some minor heat exhaustion (mostly the northerners), some complaints about the waiting time (mostly by the prissier of the actors), and how locked in the vehicles were (mostly by the media who wanted to leave as soon as the photo ops collapsed) everyone left satisfied that their investment of time and sweat was worth the journey.

✳✳✳

Dr. Bernard Sherban attended the ceremony sporting a big goofy grin and accompanied by his fiancé (and the reason for the grin), Jane Peterson. Saundra and Nathan were also there. The party was escorted by security past cheering Aquatiacs and sneering "stars" to the VIP section where they met Manuel and Elena Gomez. Mr. Gomez remembered both Nathan and Saundra fondly from Hinson Middle School. He did a lot of little jobs for one of their favorite teachers and was in her room enough to get to know some of her students.

"You were both cute teeny little kids ... now look at you," he recollected, his soft grandfatherly accent a warm familiar memory to the teenagers.

Eduardo Two Otters (a.k.a. Cola Man) flanked by his sons was also in this section. Unlike the others who had parked at the Granada Bridge and taken the free shuttle, they had arrived in their airboat, which they had coincidentally launched from the boat ramp in same parking lot. After introductions, the men from the Everglades found it strikingly lucky that not only did they park at the same spot, but their party numbered nine, and they had brought their smaller nine passenger craft. Such luck was not to be ignored, so they offered to give all of them a ride back to their cars. The offer was gladly accepted.

Especially since the luck was three, not twofold. Their party was not originally intended to have been nine. Saundra had snuck Jessica and this week's boyfriend in, but they had disappeared soon after arriving when Jessica tore off into the crowd, boyfriend in tow. She thought she spotted her favorite singer. Saundra followed the sound of Jessica's shouts.

"CHRISTINA!

"CHRISTINA WAIT! I'M YOUR BIGGEST FAN!"

"OHMYGOD CHRISTINA, IT IS YOU ISN'T IT?!"

"CHRISTINA?!" … until they faded away. A text message on Saundra's cell phone was the last she heard of Jessica that day. It read.

> *john is such a dweeb he didn't even help me find christina who is so gone now i'll never find her and then he left angry but that's ok cause i ran into frank from algebra ii last year remember him? he says i look nice in this shirt and he wants to take me to the movies later and i can ride home with him and his uncle where he has his car and he'll take me home afterwards so don't worry and i've already called mom and she says its all right so i'm just like telling you now so you and your family don't freak … bye.*[4]

They heard a few speeches (Bernie had to give one). They "oohed" and "aahed" when the monument was unveiled, and applauded when the ribbon was cut. Bernie, Jane, Saundra Nathan, Mr. and Mrs. Gomez, Eduardo and his sons bailed out soon after. Crowding into the airboat they covered their ears as the giant fan blades whirred into action. The Two Otters Clan men navigated the waters to their cars by hugging the shore to avoid waves, the mortal enemy of these boats[5]. This made the ride infinitely safer, but longer, because they had to watch for rocks[6]. No one complained; quite the contrary in fact. There was no hurry, the time did not matter, and the moist breeze felt good on this hot day. For them, the event was over. There would be plenty of opportunities to see the center when the crowds died down.

At the boat ramp, they all helped the sons of Mr. Two Otters with cleaning the boat, and securing it on the trailer. The day was winding down, and they were hungry. Jane proposed to buy everyone dinner. The Gomezes were going out anyway, so they agreed. The Two Otter men had a long drive, and indicated they would be grateful for a free meal as long as it served strong coffee, was close to I-95, and there was a large parking lot for their tow.

They met at Chili's.

The staff welcomed Mr. and Mrs. Gomez with the affection of a family visit. They arranged a nice table for the eclectic group. The nine enjoyed a good meal and better conversations.

Somewhere in the meal, Manuel asked Bernie, "Professor, where do you intend to seek answers next?"

"Actually Mr. Gomez, I've decided to take some time off from research to dedicate myself more to teaching. I've been on the move constantly for two solid years, and quite frankly Mr. Gomez … I am beat."

"But what of your fiancé professor? She will be so far away," teased Mrs. Gomez.

"Jane's working with me. The Florida Park Service and the university have enterered a joint venture, Mrs. Gomez," Bernie explained. "Jane and I have been assigned the task of sifting through the historical artifacts of the early Florida colonies for *Homo aquaticus* clues. There's a possibility that a settler might have written or illustrated something in a letter, diary or family Bible, that would provide answers to some of our questions. Maybe their descendants locked away a vital artifact, thinking of it as only a useless heirloom.

"We have an enormous database to study. Cracker items alone will preoccupy us for years. Then there are archives from runaway slaves and other settlers. Most of the artifacts are stored in a Miami warehouse," Bernie added.

"So you're both moving to Miami, then?" Manuel said, grinning.

"Yes, for a few years. At least until this line of research collapses," said Bernie. "But eventually, Jane and I'll be up here. We have work at the center that will fill many years of research life. I've grown to love the Ormond Beach area very much. It is my strongest intention to eventually break my ties with Miami and live here permanently."

"Why not now?" pressed Manuel, "Surely the artifacts you and Ms. Peterson will analyze can be transported."

"Because," Bernie replied, glancing over at Saundra, "I hear the freshman class at the university is quite formidable this fall." he smiled.

From the far end of the table, Saundra nodded her head appreciatively.

"Dr. Sherban?" the Cola Man spoke. He had apparently been waiting patiently for a lull in the chatter to make an inquiry. Interrupting was out of the question for the old man, so he had monitored the dialogue much like a pedestrian trying to traverse a busy intersection monitored traffic.

"Mr. Two Otters, please. Call me Bernie" he said.

"OK, then. My friends call me Eddy Two," he replied.

"Can I—" Nathan, attempting to interrupt.

"No," responded Saundra and Jane simultaneously. Saundra followed the conversational smack down with a smothering kiss.

"Bernie, then," Cola Man continued. "I always kinda had a problem puttin' stuff together. Not *real* stuff. Stuff I can get my fingers on? Now that's a cinch. Gimme a jigsaw, or an old engine, and I can make 'em right in a jiffy. It's pictures in my head I can't seem to reconcile. Always has been. I guess that's why school and me didn't get along. I know my grandmother's story was related to Sabatez and Namor all right. I'm sure of that ... I just can't seem to fit the pieces right."

"You're wondering what Talimiqua has to do with Namor and Sabatez?" Bernie asked.

"Yeah. That's about it," Cola Man replied.

The table chatter dropped significantly in anticipation of Bernie's reply. That was a question they all wondered about.

"The short answer is that I honestly have no idea ... "

Silence ... broken finally by Saundra.

"Lame!" she declared. "You so *absolutely* do know. You're just hedging because of your stupid 'professional restraint.' C'mon Bernie. You're in good company. No one here is going to call you on this ... How are they connected?"

Bernie looked on the faces of his dinner companions. Saundra was indeed right. He was in good company. And damn her, she was also right that he was reflexively holding back his thoughts because he hadn't completely worked them out.

But wasn't that what good academicians were *supposed* to do? Shouldn't a supposed expert have his thoughts resolved before blurting them out for the world to scrutinize? Nevertheless, Bernie couldn't help but feel stupid even as he thought this. These people weren't critics. He wasn't being asked as an expert.

A gentle old man had merely asked him for a clarification. He would not judge Bernie poorly if it turned out to be erroneous. For that matter, none of these people would.

So, emitting the quietest of sighs (which only Jane acknowledged by squeezing his knee affectionately) Bernie answered Eddy Two.

"My best hunch, Mr.—" Bernie paused and corrected himself. "Pardon me ... Eddy Two, is that Talimiqua was a Calusan concoction. Too many variables have to align for the story to be otherwise. If that's the case, then Sabatez likely forced the tribe he attacked to flee. They could have been wary of the pirates' return or maybe their numbers were so reduced that they retreated inland. Who knows?

"Maybe there was a rift between the land and the water tribes. The motivation isn't something I'm too sure about, and no goading by Saundra is going to change that. What I *am* confident is guessing that they somehow wound up in a Calusa tribe—probably captured and absorbed. Given what they went through, they wouldn't have been able to put up much of a fight.

"Interbreeding between the two merged tribes would dilute the presence of the *homo aquaticus* manifestation, but it would still occur. Knowing what they were capable of producing, it's not hard to imagine the old tribe insisting on a secluded birth. They probably invented the Talimiqua story as a cover to go off alone to the water. Over time, there were fewer and fewer "water children" births, but the stories remained. The tribes forgot who was absorbed and who was there before. All they knew was their lore," Bernie concluded.

"So the assimilated Calusans invented Talimiqua?" Jane asked.

"I think they did," Bernie acknowledged softly, "yes."

"That'd push the time frame well into the sixteenth or even the seventeenth centuries." Jane exclaimed.

"I think it would, yes … Maybe even later," Bernie acknowledged, even more softly. Clearly this was uncomfortable territory for him.

"So what stopped the *homo aquaticus* gene?" Saundra chimed in.

"Bernie?" Jane prodded, when her fiancé wouldn't reply.

"Who says it stopped?" came the softest answer Bernie had ever uttered.

"The Calusans must have seriously outnumbered the remaining tribe members, so the infusion of so much new genetic material would have diluted the expression, but some *Homo aquaticus* had to have been born or the Talimiqua legend would never have arisen. I'm certain of that … I just don't know how strong the gene was," Bernie added, in an attempt to defend his obviously controversial reply.

Eddy Two absorbed Bernie's answer patiently for about a minute. The table ate silently, allowing him the space to digest it.

Then Eddy Two began to chuckle. His body rumbled with an inner mirth he was truly enjoying and, while his hardened face did not reveal it, the oscillations of the table bumps were jovial and amplifying.

Without knowing why, the rest of the table joined in on the laugh.

"What is the joke, Father?" one of his sons finally asked.

"Seems that Namor's DNA came into my tribe and stayed. One of you two could have been a fish man," he replied, the barest hint of a smile cracking the creased lips of his leathery face.

That reactivated the laughter. Amidst the good humor, Saundra excused herself and left for the restroom. As she navigated the maze of tables and chairs to her destination, she leaned over to Bernie and whispered, "He's right isn't he? Someone might still be making *aquaticus*. That's why you're so uncomfortable with this subject."

Bernie nodded his head ever so slightly and Saundra retreated.

The meal ended, the eclectic entourage bid each other fond farewells, split into their three respective groups and went their separate ways. Bernie and Jane made a mental note to become as comfortable with one another as the Gomeze's. Nathan went online that night and applied to the University of Miami's School of Performing Arts. Eddy Two considered telling his sons about the other stories his wild grandmother had told him, but the events of the day, his large meal, and the hum of the engine got the better of him.

He fell asleep.

Saundra still couldn't get the Calusas that fled to Cuba out of her mind.

CHAPTER
12

Tish and Maru

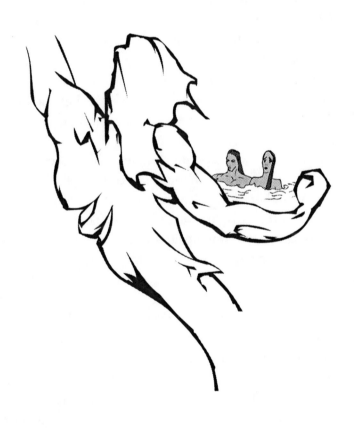

The pilgrimage was typically a three day investment. Neither Tish, nor Maru liked the shallows at all, so they were determined to make it in one. This meant beginning their journey early, well before the sun's sheen glistened on the surface above, which in turn required traveling by day through dense land tribe regions. As a precaution, they each harvested eight large silt dwelling sea cucumbers, mucking themselves with the sticky gray secretion they released when agitated. It was a light coat, easily applied, with an altogether not very unpleasant fragrance, and even more easily scraped off. It itched a little. To truly transform their two toned brown skin to gray, they should have used ten, but the disguise need only fool the lazy land kin eye, so they didn't bother being as thorough.

The reward for their early start, and skin irritation would be the darkness protecting them when they reached their destination.

Tonight would be an excellent opportunity for the pilgrimage. Tides favored them, the moon was full and the sky clear. They ate a light meal, so as not to cramp up, and set off for their long swim at a hard pace covering the open waters to the mainland in the time it took the sun to reach zenith. The remarkable speed of this first leg of their journey was not unexpected. Few in the Tribe could match Tish and Maru on long swims. The day of their wedding, the running joke was that their children would have the ability to explore the world and still be on time for supper.

With the shoreline, and the inlet in sight, the pilgrims paused briefly to recharge. They did not trust the fish living so close to the shore, so Maru had passed by his friend Ree's storeroom and packed a lunch for them in his pouch. Ree was a much better food preparer than either he or Tish, and this day was special. Maru promised to replenish the stores the moment he returned. Tish, recognizing Ree's handiwork, attacked the meal as soon as Maru handed it to her. She enjoyed the leaf wrap around her fish. Maru, ever the connoisseur, did not think it properly accented the meat's flavor, so he cast it off. They ate in silence, enjoying the companionship. Each was lost in their private thoughts, but they both mulled the same notion.

This was fun.

As children, they had traveled on long swims nearly every day. Few enjoyed the freedom it granted, or rather, few were willing to make the investment to earn that freedom. Long swims meant pumping the tail in smooth rhythmic sweeps at three quarters strength for half a day or more. Arms were held tightly at their sides, dorsals erect, stabilizing and streamlining their form to maximize their thrust. Mouths locked painfully wide open exploiting their cut through the waters, gill slits expanded.

Like a shark, if they moved fast enough, they would not have to bellows their ribcage. Their very motion would force enough water through to fuel their blood. Maintaining this rigid form for long periods required discipline, a powerful physique, and an independent spirit. Since the oceans were so vast, and most of the people were quite content to linger near the Tribe, long swimmers typically had little company but their own. As such, long swimmers were usually loners. That was what made Maru and Tish unique. They were the paradox— Social long swimmers.

They had explored every one and two day long swim listed in the great plaza. They had even discovered a few so distant, seasons later, artists were still awaiting confirmation to seed them on the large map.

When they advanced to a courtship, the journeys continued, but less frequently. After their wedding, they were lucky if they had the opportunity to try one each moon cycle. How ironic that their mutual passion shriveled as their relationship grew. How ever more ironic that it was their decision to have children which reengaged them on their first true long swim since their return to the Tribe after their wedding. Spontaneously, and nearly in unison, Maru and Tish turned to one another and said:

"We should never have stopped this."

They smiled, finding it funny, but unsurprising that they were thinking so similarly. Tish had packed the cleaning sticks. A few tooth scrubs and a quick spin to dislodge any food stuffs, and they were off again.

They followed the tide's swell in, breaking form upon breaching the artificially narrow inlet, running the oily waters through their lungs in short bellows until they were well up river and clear of the foul contaminants. Then travel slowed. Long swim form was difficult to maintain in narrow environments, but their delay was mostly because of Tish. Tribe materials were quite different than those of the land kin. They were for the most part, less colorful, sturdier, and rougher. Tish particularly enjoyed the incredibly smooth surface textures. She'd rub against them at every opportunity, sliding her back and tail around bridge pylons, wooden dock posts, metal buoys, and especially the boat hulls. She spun and turned vigorously to feel the smoothness all over. Maru was constantly scolding her that not only was she in danger of revealing her presence, but the rubbing would remove her camouflage. She playfully ignored him until a large ship nearly sucked her into the vortex it created behind itself. She clung desperately to Maru who clung even more desperately to a rock until the vacuum moved on. She did not drift again.

The Tribe Map plotted their destination quite nicely. It was one of the oldest locations on record. So old was it in fact that it was one of three places the tenders removed coral polyps to maintain the appropriate shape, rather than seeding to build structure. They knew roughly where to go, but getting there was another matter. Seeing was difficult in these churned narrow waters. Hearing was even worse. The constant whine of so many of their boats disoriented them. Their friend Sall, a very spiritual man, had made the trip with his wife Salea six times now. He had told them of a deep land kin channel carved so their big ships would not flounder along the center of the river. Sall advised that their best course should be to follow it. He did not know how many bridges upriver the destination was because they kept making so many, but he did mention that they would know when they were near because the surface dwellings on the sunset shore would be replaced by forest. Even that he was not certain of since dwellings also rose so rapidly.

To their knowledge, Sall and Salea had been the last to have made the pilgrimage, and their youngest child was already in school. Tish and Maru's inquiries could find no more recent venturers. The comforts of the Tribe were apparently too enticing for most couples to leave it merely to embark through a sludgy land kin infested regions in honor of what they considered to be only superstitious nonsense anyway. Tish and Maru did not see it as nonsense. One could not explore their world as extensively as they without garnering a reverence for the spirituality of places. They were nonetheless uncomfortable with the age of their directions.

Finding the channel was easy. Maneuvering the river between zippy boats, and plodding behemoths was not. They lost track of the bridge count. Sall was right. Many of them were not only new, they were constructed at locations where the old bridge remnants still stood. Taking turns poking out on the surface to check for the forest, Maru finally spied the last house, as the moon rose.

Boat traffic had dwindled considerably, their silence a welcome respite. Sediments calmed, and the river took on a more natural appearance. They tasted trace sweetness. A fresh water river's content was seeping in, mingling with the saltiness.

They were near.

Holding hands for strength as the importance of their journey became real, Maru and Tish maneuvered closer to shore seeking the ancient marker gouged into the river bottom. It would be hidden by silt of course, but they had a general idea where to concentrate their search. Again, Sall had provided good counsel.

"You will come across a string of narrow islands. They are land kin constructs and easy to identify. Follow them around the bend just beyond their boat storage corral. The marker is between there and the tiny bridge leading to the sweet water river. Kai rests in the shallows between the last island and the shore. The bones are exposed, but silt covered. Find the marker. It will show you exactly where."

Sall added that the area quickly deserted as the evening's darkness deepened. Even if a straggler or two wandered the shore, hardly a surface light at all flickered, and certainly none pierced the water. They would have plenty of privacy for their prayers.

"Stop worrying so much. Go pay your respects to Kai. Then come home and start making husbands for my six daughters."

Sall's casual approach to long swims irked them both. He was too cavalier of the risks involved. His safe journeys were a testimonial for sheer blundering good fortune, and Salea's powerful muscles, more than anything else. But his advice was factually reliable, and no one could ever really get angry at Sall.

Turning the bend after the last of the islands, they reached the general location, or at least they thought they did. The description did not at all match. Sall had stressed it was isolated, dark, and quite peaceful. Clear of the island's shading, it was evident that this place was none of that. Land kin lights blazed through the waters, igniting everything from surface to bottom— most definitely including them— with a white sheen. Rumbles of the motorized boat traffic shook every water droplet. And there were land kin... Many many land kin. Amassed in large numbers wandering the shores, the light was so bright, and their eyes were not very effective out of the water, but it appeared they were mostly looking out in their direction. They dared not remain, and quickly receded to the shadows. From there, they risked a cautious poke out the surface.

And they saw it.

Mounted on the very soil where the Great Kai rested, nearly half as tall as the surrounding trees, basking in land kin lighting, a statue stood.

Immense, white, surrounded by stylized dolphins of the same color and texture, an intricate sculpture of a fully extended water child leaping from the waves, one arm stretched up to the sky, face locked in jubilant celebration rose from the shore. It was quite beautiful actually. Maru and Tish never found their marker, but they were relatively certain, the statue rose precisely from the Tribe's most hallowed ground. Surprise and wonder initially overpowered them and they were taken aback by the majesty. Then realization crept in, and despite their position in the shadows, they both suddenly felt very exposed, and sank below the surface, cautiously retreating to the darker open river, often glancing back nervously. Tish in particular seemed disturbed by what she had seen. Maru worried for her, but knew his wife well enough to wait until they had retreated to a safely isolated position before attempting to converse. An excruciatingly silent swim later, they found a deep pocket in the river's channel and, anchoring their tails to a pair of boulders, they turned to one another.

"That looks NOTHING like Kai!" Tish blurted, skipping many many steps in the conversation.

Maru, a patient methodical thinker, could not leap that far ahead and was unable to respond at first. Tish was right of course. The statue must have been a rendition of the great Kai, whose obvious differences in appearance from the original were unquestionably stark. Kai's bones must have been discovered. There was always speculation that this would occur. Ancestors had taken the precaution of maneuvering the waters to submerge the grave but it was always vulnerably close to the shore.

The land kin seemed dissatisfied with an entire continent to settle. More and more often they had invaded the waters to create land simply to feed their ravenous construction. Over the years, the council had reviewed a regular stream of submitted proposals to salvage Kai's remains from the land kin machinery. One creative thinker had even suggested a water tunnel (A fine idea, but one impossible to implement clandestinely.) The Tribe did have some air breathing allies. Representatives of the true land kin descendants still met for one council each year. There were those few who through unique circumstances had known of them, and vowed to keep their secret. There were also the giants of the cold continent. All at one point had been suggested as rescuers. All suggestions had been politely rejected. Maru remembered how upset those whose warnings were disparaged felt afterwards. There will be many others as well who remember the proposals and who will judge the council harshly. He worried that the imminent danger facing the Tribe now would be subverted by an even more powerful desire to seek justice for the council's apparently wrong course. Their inaction had created the two greatest dangers in his lifetime, and quite possibly in the life of the Tribe.

Kai's grave had been dug up by the land kin, but much worse was the second;

The land kin knew of them.

"MARU!"

Tish gripped his shoulders with both hands jostling him back to the present.

"Maru, I said it looks nothing like Kai." She repeated. A slight tremble in her voice the only indication that her worry was as keen as his.

Maru thought of the statue's appearance. Despite the repercussions it created, he admitted being genuinely impressed with the workmanship. The statue did bear a striking resemblance to their kind, and it was cast in a flattering pose. And once he got past the huge mistake, there were some physical similarities. He could see bits of Kai in the statue.

"Yes it does." he replied sincerely.

"What's wrong with it?" he added, knowing full well the answer. Tish was dumbfounded. "WHAT?"

"I mean, besides the obvious mistake, what else is wrong? You have to give them credit Tish, they made a pretty good guess."

"What? No! No... No they didn't. Ok, forgetting the obvious FOR THE MOMENT, the hair is all wrong, and the hands, what are those things between the fingers?"

"Webbing... I think... THEY think we have webbed hands." Maru tried responding, but Tish was not listening.

"And how could they possibly believe our great spiritual leader could have moved with such renowned lightning speed using that stump of a small tail?"

"All they had were the bones Tish. Bones and lore. Give them credit for the honor they granted."

Tish had to admit the land people had done right to mark the Great Kai's burial site with an appropriate marker.

"But Maru, it is so wrong!"

"Mistakes happen. They misunderstood the bones, or the lore, or whatever they discovered. It doesn't matter. What is important is that they are aware of us. And judging by the monument, they do not hold us in a bad light. But we must report to the council."

"Yes… but not quite yet Maru." Tish said in an unusually timid voice.

"I still want to ask for Kai's blessing on our child." She added even softer.

Maru loved Tish. He had loved her since they were children. That love never had and never would dwindle. There were times however when the quantity of love gushed in great swabs and he was humbled to be so lucky as to have been selected as the recipient of the love of one so wonderful.

This was one of those gushing times.

They cautiously made their way as close to the statue as they dared. The lights were annoying, but they found shadows to maneuver through. They came to within a three jump length, and could not go further because of the shallows. Circling around hoping to approach from the other side of the island proved futile. A wall of forest litter clogged the water.

So this is what exposed Kai. The marker was probably smothered underneath the pile.

They returned to their closest view and broke the surface. Keeping their mouths tightly shut allowing the bilging of the life giving water in and out of their rib slits, they could in silence enjoy the view. Maru took Tish's hand in his.

Despite it all, here was the Great Kai's grave. Kai's remains, unlike any other of the Tribe were intact. Kai's unrelenting courage and love even in death provided inspiration for them all. Couples intent on having children made the pilgrimage to Kai's final resting place since the time of the Great Rift. They spoke a prayer under the surface, and in deference to the Gifts the land had so generously provided those many seasons ago, they would return the generosity with a gift of their own. Tish pulled her pack open and removed the pearl pendant her mother had given her as a reward for completing her schooling. She and Maru gripped the pearl. They could not speak without submerging, but they did not have to. Each said the prayer in their minds while holding the gaze of the other. They finished it in unison, and Tish tossed the pearl at the statue. She had a good throwing arm. It bounced off the shoulder and dropped somewhere in the grass.

They looked on in silence for a while longer, and without consulting each other, simultaneously flipped down to begin their trek home. They held hands as they swam. It was Tish who first spoke, and that was not until they traversed the river and were out in the open seas. Once she began, she did not stop until they reached the Tribe. Maru endured her tirade. He understood this was how Tish released stress, and although he would never tell her, she did take on a beautiful glow when she was angry. Besides what could he do… argue?

Tish had the truth on her side. Maru had defended the statue because he understood the disadvantage the artists were working under. But he had to admit, despite the land kin's best effort, the big error they made overpowered any subsequent similarities.

The statue was not Kai. It couldn't be her.

"Where was HER spear?" Tish went on, "And HER hair was much longer and tied with a shell. Everyone knows that. And that puny tail! How could SHE possibly have leapt out of the water with such a stump! The Great Kai, MOTHER of the Tribe indeed."

She arrived at the Tribe so hoarse from her complaining, Maru had to do all the talking when they interrupted the council. The seven elders listened patiently. They asked many questions and adjourned to discuss the matter. Maru and Tish were accosted by friends and neighbors afterwards and they recanted their discovery several more times before escaping into the privacy of their home. Outside, the Tribe was teeming with the excited chatter of the new development. A barrier with the land kin had been irreparably shattered. Uncertain days lay ahead. Only time would reveal whether they would be good or dangerous.

Tish and Maru decided that they would wait a little while before having children.

***

The Granada Bridge spans the Halifax River, connecting mainland Ormond Beach with the beachside. Each footprint of the bridge sports a tiny park where pedestrians can enjoy the river. Fishermen, joggers, and lovers can be found at all hours enjoying the resource.

This night, from high on the bridge, a couple out on a moonlight stroll, spotted Tish and Maru as they swam underneath.

"Ooh look Bill! Do you see that!"

Bill acknowledged that he did.

They watched in fascination until the merman and mermaid disappeared under the bridge.

Stunned into silence by the site, it was the woman who finally spoke;

"God, I think dolphins are the most beautiful creatures on this planet, don't you agree?"

Bill acknowledged that he did and they continued on their way.

The End

Endnotes

CHAPTER 1

1 Wikipedia is a Web-based, free content encyclopedia that is openly edited and freely readable. The source for the above definition appropriately enough is www.wikipedia.org.

2 On the river, at the southwest foot of the town's only bridge spanning the Intercoastal to the beaches.

3 Clowns in the circus are what they bring out to entertain the audience while the next important show is cued up...

4 How many ways could "hot with 3pm thunderstorms" be said?

5 I-75 on the West coast; I-95 on the East Coast ... I-10 technically takes people out, but to do that a driver has to traverse the deceptively long length of the Florida Panhandle. And it dumps into the coastal areas of Alabama and Mississippi ... Which aren't much safer.

6 A note must be made here that Jeanne was a murderous storm. The damage to Florida was mostly a financial disaster, but other places weren't quite so fortunate. Haiti alone suffered more than 1,500 deaths.

CHAPTER 2

1 Lawyer definition of *pro bono* — "I'll get my money from someone BESIDES you."

2 From *Spanish* — "No, it is still one island."

3 From *Spanish* — "How interesting, the fresh water sterilized the rocks."

4 So, unless this was a Spanish soldier, a Soviet spy, or Al Gore, he was out of luck.

5 From *Spanish* — "My God, this cannot be!"

6 He was right.

7 He was wrong ... It's the "fibula."

8 From *Spanish* — "But to what can I compare this to?"

9 Weeki Wachee Springs. Founded in 1947 by a navy frogman named Newton Perry. Perry developed a technique for putting on shows underwater via a tube attached to an air compressor. He called the concept "hose breathing," dressed a bunch of pretty girls as mermaids and a tourist phenomena was born. As of this writing, Weeki Wachee is struggling financially, but still open.

10 From *Spanish* — "Mermaid!"

11 From *Spanish* — "What am I going to do with you Little Mermaid?"

12 From *Spanish* — "Well, at least you've given me an interesting story to tell Elena tonight."

13 From *Spanish* — "Hopefully you lived well little mermaid."

CHAPTER 3

1 From *Spanish* — "Pretty strong."

2 Florida State's football stadium. Where the Seminoles play very well ...
Unless of course they're playing Miami.

3 And their presence at this apparent historic event.

4 From *Spanish* — "the mermaid."

5 FYI: The nerd word for the chemical is "bufotenine."

6 It wasn't ... They DID lick the toads, and they DID hallucinate, but they
used all sorts of other drugs too. The Mayan high priests had "issues." For
more details, do a Google search using the key words "Maya, toad,
hallucinogen." Or in a shameless, unsolicited plug for my old boss who
introduced me to the whole frog licking/Maya connection, buy and read:
Lee, Julian. *The Field Guide to the Amphibians and Reptiles of the Maya World*.
Ithaca, NY and London: Cornell University Press, 2000.

7 Take I-4 to State Road 92; Take 92 to Beach Street; Take Beach Street to the
Main Street Bridge; Go over the bridge and park the car ... You can't miss it!

8 *Pupae*. The third of four insect life cycle stages—egg, larva, pupae, adult—
which in butterflies involves the cocoon.

9 But NOT a date!

10 Because it WASN'T a date.

11 Ground Penetrating Radar (GPR). A technique for determining the
composition of nonmetallic materials invented in the 1920's that gets better
and better as computers get faster. Typically, a cart rolls over an area
bombarding radio waves into the ground. A receiver monitors and records
any interference. Computers take the interference and compare it to a
database of known resistances, and then they generate an image of what's
underneath. GPR was first used successfully to map the inside of ice fields.
As the ability to crunch the huge gobs of numbers generated improved,
archeology exploited it to map buried crypts, city walls, sunken ships, etc.
The military is working with GPR to map minefields. Municipalities use it to
find power lines and old architecture. GPR was an integral tool at ground
zero where the World Trade Center once stood.

12 Electromagnetic Survey. This technique specifically targets finding buried
metals. A pole generates an electrical current that (depending on the strength
and pole size) penetrates the ground to a specific depth. Pickups record the
fluctuations in the current and again, computers crunch the numbers.
Electromagnetic Surveys can be handheld (Utility workers employ them to
find metal cable lines) or they can be large enough to attach to helicopters for
surveying the metallic content of large swabs of land.

CHAPTER 4

1 From *The Hitchhiker's Guide to the Galaxy* by Douglas Adams(1978-79). If you haven't read it, please put this book down and do so. In fact, read everything the late Mr. Adams wrote … I'll wait.

2 The position of choice for textbook drawings — on its back, facing forward, palms out.

3 Search for Extra Terrestrial Intelligence program (SETI@home) designed as a screen saver. The plan is to tap the unused processor power of thousands of idle, but running computers. Data gathered from telescopes pointed at various points in the sky is broken down to small chunks and sent to participants with the program running. Each time their screen saver pops up, some of it is crunched, and the results are passed along the internet to a central location. A pretty clever idea, if you ask me. If you want to participate, go to http://setiathome.ssl.berkeley.edu/download.html.

4 Bones are alive. They respond to stress by growing. The more they're stressed, the stronger they grow. Bones are stressed at the tendons, where muscle attaches, and over years a bump called a tuberocity forms. The larger the tuberocity, the more vigorous that bone's stress was. Skeletons of infants and kings for example are quite smooth and bump free since they did not endure very much labor. Slave skeletons on the other hand bear impressive tuberocities. The left hand of the merman must have been "bumpier."

5 Coconut Grove. An artists' community along Biscayne Bay with great restaurants, expensive stores and an amazing art festival every year.

CHAPTER 5

1 Male and female skeletons vary the most at the pelvis. Female pelvises are broader, with the hip crests turned outward to accommodate the womb during pregnancy. Male pelvises, unburdened with the reproduction requirement, are significantly narrower.
   Namor's pelvis is hardly more than an expanded vertebra, rendering this traditional identification technique useless.

2 Around 6'2"

3 *Homo sapiens* — The species which identifies all intelligent humans who ever lived. It includes Neanderthal, Cro-Magnon, and us, and translates to the rather arrogant "Man the Wise."

4 *Homo sapiens sapiens* — The SUBspecies of homo sapiens that distinguishes modern humans from our less refined ancestors and translates to the rather grammatically silly "Man the Wise Wise."

5   Carbon Dating 101. Nitrogen in the air is constantly exposed to cosmic rays. These rays smash neutrons into the Nitrogen atoms converting them to a high energy form of Carbon with 14 particles in its nucleus (C^{14}). C^{14} is unstable and over time breaks down to boring, stable C^{12}, but there is a bunch of Nitrogen in the atmosphere, and lots and lots of cosmic rays, so this process is continuously renewing C^{14}. Plants absorb this C^{14} as Carbon dioxide. Animals eat plants, and bacteria eat EVERYTHING. Pretty much every living thing therefore has a certain percentage of C^{14}, and they're constantly renewing their supply… until they die. Then they stop renewing … because they're dead. The C^{14} that breaks down never gets replaced. What makes C^{14} a useful dating tool is that the breakdown is steady and predictable. In 5,730 years approximately half the C^{14} is gone. In about 40,000 years it's all gone, transforming into boring, stable C^{12}. Scientists can therefore determine how old any living thing was when the "living" part ended by figuring out how much C^{14} is present. The more there is, the younger the find. You, the reader, for example, are saturated with C^{14} but dinosaur bones have none.

6   Roughly 220 – 240 lbs.

7   *Facial Reconstruction.* The art of "fleshing out" a skull to show what the owner looked like in life. Originally done by applying clay directly on the skull using measurements of several "landmark" spots established by a guy named Mikhail Gerasimov (inspiring a pretty good, but kind of gross book called *Gorky Park* written by Martin Cruz Smith … They made a movie too, but the book's a lot better.) Today, computers and 3D scanners have replaced the sculptor, but to Gerasimov's credit, they still employ his numbers.

8   Human ribcages consist of twelve pairs of ribs. The top ten attach to the sternum (chestplate) with a chunk of cartilage, hence their grouping as "attached." The lowest two do not connect, and are often referred to as "floating" ribs.

9   *Intercostals.* Muscles between the ribs whose function is to expand the ribcage. They're what you eat if you have barbequed ribs.

10   The pointy part of your spine that you feel along the midline of your back.

11   There are 3 types of vertebrae making up all vertebrate spines:

Cervical: From where the head attaches to the ribs … In short — the neck. These vertebrae are the smallest and most flexible of the three because they're holding up and moving the head.

Thoracic: all the ones with ribs jutting from them.

Lumbar: the lower vertebrae, fatter than the others, because they support more of the torso.

12   Dorsals act like the feathers on an arrow. They streamline the medium they're zipping through so the projectile won't spiral out of control. In the case of arrows, this keeps their trajectory predictable. Animals have the ability to compensate when they career off course, but that'd take energy. Why would they bother constantly spending that energy straightening themselves out when a jutting fin or two could do it?

13   There are two classes of fish — Cartilaginous (sharks, rays, and skates) and Bony (Pretty much every fish that ISN'T a shark, ray, or skate)

14   Finger bones.

15   On the back

16   Toe bones… I KNOW the other reference said fingers. Phalanges refer to those bones that extend from the base of a hand, foot, paw, etc…

17   Tarsal and Metatarsals: Ankle and foot bones

18   On the front

19   Tiffany Yorks is a beautiful, charming 16-year-old living in Florida. In 1989, in Tampa Florida's Shriner's Hospital, she was a beautiful, charming newborn with Mermaid's Syndrome. Surgeons separated the legs when she was a few months old, and she is still undergoing corrective operations, but by all accounts she is living a normal life.

Milagros Cerron was born in Peru in 2004. She had two fused legs, but each had independent movement and bone structure. She only has one kidney, and digestive tract complications, but was otherwise complete. Milagros is scheduled to begin the gauntlet of procedures that Tiffany went through on February 24, 2005. (The author's hopes and good wishes extend to her and her family.) Run a Google search for "Sirenomelia" along with each child's name for updates.

20   Occam's Razor. A rule conjured up by a guy named William of Occam. It states that if two or more EQUALLY plausible scenarios exist, the simplest is true. It's the science version of "tie goes to the runner".

21   *Hypothermia:* losing more heat than you can afford.

22   *Sternum:* chest bone

23   Water breathers pull dissolved oxygen gas (O_2) from water. O_2 gets in the water two ways: churning surface conditions like waves, ripples and splashes trap it, and photosynthetic organisms such as plants and algae make it.

A common water breather misconception is that they rip the *"O"* from "H_2O." They can't do that.

24   Atmospheric O_2 accounts for 28% of inhaled air or about 200,000*ppm* (parts per million). Dissolved O_2 in fertile waters hovers around 10*ppm* and can't be greater than that without triggering dangerous bacteria blooms. Namor's physiology would therefore have to have come up with approximately 20,000 fold improvement.

25 The ability of a thumb to reach across the hand and touch the pinky.

26 Torpor: an autopilot state where an aquatic mammal still moves through the water, comes up for air, etc. But isn't conscious — it's sort of "sleep swimming"

27 "Closed Population" is a term used by geneticists to describe a group with no immigration or emigration. Offspring come solely from the members within that population. All genetic traits—good or bad—therefore tend to spread to the entire population. Deer living on a remote island are a good example of a closed population. Their numbers change only as a result of births and deaths. Rats living in an abandoned building are not. New rats constantly trickle in. Some rats are either forced out, or they wander on their own to other more lucrative rat habitats… like the dumpster or another abandoned building.

28 Between 50 and 97% of the human code, depending on the article you read.

CHAPTER 6

1 IB: *I*nternational *B*accalaureate is a grueling academic program designed to produce a well rounded college student. Similar (and depending on the institution sometimes superior) to the AP academies, IB is different in that it requires proficiency in all subjects, rather than allowing for specialization solely in the student's strength. It was created as an accreditation system to allow foreign educated students quicker access to American Universities. Good IB high school programs produce well prepared collegians with up to thirty college credits.

CHAPTER 8

1 From *Spanish*, "Sun Coast." The term used to describe Spain's beaches from the City of Malaga to Gibraltar.

CHAPTER 9

1 Nocoroco was decimated mostly from European diseases imported by the Spaniards and the French. Its population dropped from an estimated 13,000 in 1560 to virtually disappearing in the 1700's. The shell mounds within Tomoka State Park in Ormond Beach and a few artifacts are all that remains.

2 From *Spanish*, "pastries" and "croquettes." The former is a flaky Cuban concoction stuffed with guava, cheese, ground beef, ham, or whatever else is lying around the kitchen. Each "pastel" flavor is shape specific. Guava pastels are rectangles, ground beef is circular, ham triangular, etc. As for croquettes, they are deep fried corn meal and meat amalgams that are the closest to ambrosia any food has ever achieved. The two best places for *croquetas* are the Royal Palm Bodega in Miami, on South West Eighth Street and 58th avenue, and my mother in law's house.

3   A bodega is a little grocery store. *A very* little grocery store. Bodegas sell quick stuff—coffee, candy, pastries, etc. In Miami, they're everywhere.

4   That's why it's called *TAMIAMI* ... *TA*mpa *MIAMI* ... Get it?

5   Before it became a "pretty" road, this East/West connecting path was narrow, shoulder-less, and aptly named "Alligator Alley." Only travel-hardened Floridians and clueless tourists ever dared traverse it. The first sign upon entering the West end was "Prison, Next Right" followed by another sign reading, "Danger, Panther Crossing" and the various warnings against molesting alligators ... A few miles in, the last sign simply read "No Turns, 48 miles" ... Ask any old Floridian if they ever drove Alligator Alley and sit back. Cause we all have, and EVERYONE has a story...

FYI, mine is simple. My uncle, along with dozens of other motorists was stuck out there for several hours because a twelve foot alligator straddled both lanes, deciding that the road was a great place to sunbathe and no one dared tell it otherwise.

6   For more recent updates on the clean up progress run a Google search for "Everglades clean up." Also check "Acceler8." This was a push by Governor Jeb Bush to speed up the process which, as of 2004, was two years behind schedule.

7   Krome is another name for 177th Avenue which is technically the Western border of Miami (although a very porous border with quite a few prominent breaches). Beyond it lies nothing but Everglades... supposedly. Miami streetscape is a grid where avenues travel North/South, and Streets East/West. Krome is, therefore, 177 streets over from the heart of the city. It is a suburb of a suburb of a suburb.

8. Bureau of Indian Affairs.

CHAPTER 11

1   Catch 22: From Joseph Heller's classic novel (1961) of the same name. It's the trick the army used in this very good, sometimes hilarious, but dark story to keep soldiers from leaving the army by claiming insanity. Asking to leave the army because you were insane was a rational decision because only an insane person would *want to stay*. Hence the "asker" *couldn't* be insane because he had asked to *leave* the army... Insane soldiers would never ask to leave... And so it goes.

In everyday use, "Catch 22" is synonymous with, but much funnier, than merely saying it's a "no win situation."

2   RADAR: an acronym (RAdio Detection And Ranging) and should be in all caps.

3   "Aquatiacs" *Homo Aquaticus* Maniacs. All the greatest obsessions have nicknames. "Dead Heads," "Trekkie," etc.

4   Jessica has a part-time job at Target just to pay her text messaging bills.

5 Airboats are designed to operate in very shallow water. They are extremely top-heavy which isn't a problem as long as they remain level. The Everglades swamps and marshland are so shallow, waves don't have the volume to become an issue. Airboats can even go over soft land and grasses.

6 Airboat thrust comes from a huge fan — the larger the better. The physics behind airboat movement is simple: Grab SO MUCH air with the blades that it's less effort to push the boat forward, than to throw the air back. Air isn't very dense though, so the lighter the boat, the better this works. Airboats, therefore, have thin hulls because they go over mostly soft things— water, mud, grass, sand, alligators, ducks, etc. Rocks are lethal.

7 Cracker: A term referring to white, rural, fourth, fifth, up to eighth generation Floridians who lived here way before the state got "civilized." No one's certain how the term came to be. Theories range from the "crack" Florida cowboys made with their whip, to a poor person's technique of "cracking" corn (like the song, "Jimmy CRACK corn, and I don't care…"). My favorite is that these folks were quite rugged and living in a pretty dangerous place, so when they told stories about their daily lives and included alligators and hurricanes in one sentence, they were branded "wise-CRACKERS."

The term "cracker" has been unfairly used as a derogatory insult against Caucasians, the same way the dreaded "N-Word" is against folks of African descent … and in a silly twist, the dreaded "n-word" is also a misconception. By most accounts, its origins are from a mispronunciation of the Spanish word for "black" which is "negro" …

And around it goes.

Bibliography and References

Books regarding Native Americans

Blanchard, Charles E. *New Words, Old Songs Understanding the Lives of Ancient Peoples in Southwest Florida Through Archeology.* Gainesville, FL: 1995, Institute of Archeology and Paleoenvironmental Studies, University Press of Florida.

Hann, John H .*Missions to the Callusa.* Gainesville, FL: 1991, University Press of Florida.

Hann, John H. *A History of the Timucua Indians and Missions.* Gainesville, FL: 1996, University Press of Florida.

Ste. Clare, Dana. *True Natives: The Prehistory of Volusia County.* Datona Beach, FL: 1992, Museum of Arts and Sciences.

Worth, John F. *Timucuan Chiefdoms of Spanish Florida, Volume 1: Assimilation.* Gainesville, FL: 1998, University Press of Florida.

Worth, John F. *Timucuan Chiefdoms of Spanish Florida, Volume 2: Resistance and Destruction.* Gainesville, FL: 1998, University Press of Florida

Websites
I used the following websites to brush up on my rusty science, and verify my premises (recommended):

www.wikipedia.com
www.webmd.com

Regarding Graphics
All graphics are hand drawn by the author, mostly from memory. In those instances where memory failed me, I relied exclusively on Google Earth... My thanks to the Google folks for creating such an amazing tool.

ABOUT THE AUTHOR

Robert Hernandez was born in Havana, Cuba. He and his family escaped Castro's dictatorship and, after enduring a really cold winter in Spain, settled in Miami. Graduating with a degree in Biology from the University of Miami, Robert married his best friend, Teresa, and moved to Tampa, teaching science while she attended medical school (and he earned his Masters degree to pass the time). Robert and Dr. Teresa Hernandez have been together for twenty-five years (and counting). They spend most of their time following the exploits of their two amazing sons—Chris and Joey. After wandering all over the state, they have settled down in Ormond Beach, where they live in a long, skinny, weird house on the ocean.

Mr. Hernandez is in his third decade of teaching science in Florida. He is currently (and will hopefully forever remain) at Mainland High School.

He regularly kayaks along the Tomoka River and, while he is certain this story is a work of fiction, he occasionally probes the bottom with his oar …

Printed in the United States
125169LV00003BB/134/A